LOVE YOU SENSELESS

Susan Mac Nicol

A Men of London romance

I0553552

www.BOROUGHSPUBLISHINGGROUP.com

LOVE YOU SENSELESS
Copyright © 2014 Susan Elaine Mac Nicol

ISBN 978-1941260-80-7

To all the unsung heroes in the culinary world. To the soldiers on the battlefronts in makeshift kitchens serving up to men who themselves serve their countries. To school dinner ladies who pander to the whims of fussy schoolchildren across the world. To those serving food in homeless shelters and braving the cold to offer solace to those less fortunate perhaps than themselves. We salute you.

ACKNOWLEDGMENTS

First off, I am not a chef. I don't even like cooking. In order to write this book, I dredged up memories of my sister Cathy in her kitchen as aforementioned school dinner lady, past restaurant owner and travelling chef—ergo, when she brings her cooking to my house. And as for my Mum. well, she's an inspiration to me in this respect. I do love eating in restaurants, though, so I feel I have plenty of experience there....

As for the loss of certain senses, I was fascinated by the subject and loitered in a few forums where this was discussed. Thanks to those online who helped me out.

Thanks to the lovely JP A Bilbao who was my beta reader, offered great advice to fill in some plot holes and is a national treasure to the Philippines. Thank you, honey.

And, as always, to Jill Limber for her unerring eye in reading my work, editing it and offering me support no matter what. She is a rock star.

Contents

Chapter 1
Chapter 2
Chapter 3
Chapter 4
Chapter 5
Chapter 6
Chapter 7
Chapter 8
Chapter 9
Chapter 10
Chapter 11
Chapter 12
Chapter 13
Chapter 14
Chapter 15
Chapter 16

About the Author

LOVE YOU SENSELESS

Scorched skin and roast pork. Smells that would forever be etched into his nostrils, scraped onto the walls of his heart and mind like burning tattoos. The best thing to do would be stop smelling anything altogether so that the memory of that night could be buried deep within his psyche, never to see the light of day again. It was his only hope.

Chapter 1

The man in the bed tossed and turned as his body tried to find solace in sleep. His skin glistened with sweat and he mumbled as he thrashed among messy covers. Hands moved in agitation like those of an Italian in conversation, flapping, expressive. The sheets slipped lower on his body as his legs scissored and the covers slid off onto the floor.

He muttered a loud expletive and then gave a sharp cry. The sound echoed through the dark bedroom. His eyes opened and he stilled. For a moment, there was only the sound of his heavy breathing as he struggled to compose himself. Finally, he swung his legs out of bed and stumbled unsteadily to the en-suite bathroom. There was the sound of pissing, a steady stream that went on until the flush of the toilet. Then he made his way back to the bed where he lay, gazing up with pained eyes at the ceiling.

*****

Gideon Kent punished the piece of nicotine gum he was chewing with iron jaws. He scowled from inside the kitchen doorway of the restaurant he owned as he watched Eddie Tripp artfully place the last piece of garnish onto the dish he was plating. With a final look at the plate, like a man eyeing out a lover, Eddie picked it up and set it down on the long, heated conveyer belt that ran from one end of the stylishly designed kitchen of the restaurant to the other. The younger man watched it almost reverently as the plate made its way sedately down the belt, out into the serving area, toward hovering waiters who waited ready to pluck it up and serve it to a hopefully satisfied customer. The belt was one of Gideon's indulgences; he had seen the same practice being used in New York when he was on holiday there.

Eddie turned and whistled softly as he prepared the next plate, his hands darting like dragonflies as he skilfully picked up the ingredients to prepare yet another masterpiece. His wavy, dark red hair was held in place by a hair net, something Gideon insisted on when anyone was in the kitchen. The sous-chef had ears that were slightly larger than normal, which Gideon found endearing—why, he had no idea. Ears weren't a big turn-on for him in the usual course of things. The wide smile on Eddie's expressive, freckled face told everyone who saw him that he was enjoying himself. Gideon wanted to kiss the smile off Eddie's face and fulfil his lustful longings to pound the man into the table. He had wanted to do that about two days after the man had joined the staff of Galileo's. The red-headed man appealed to Gideon like no one had in a very long time. He didn't like the feelings Eddie caused in him, something possessive and definitely needy. It had been a little while since he had gotten laid, and craving one of his employees sucked.

"Boss? What's that look for? Is something wrong?" Carmen de Luiz, his secretary, office manager and good friend, placed a soft hand on his arm as she peered at him anxiously out of black-rimmed eyes, her black lips set in a worried curve. Gideon was used to her whole new goth look now and it no longer made him start. Carmen's lips were speckled with what looked like icing sugar and he suspected she'd been sampling the new dessert dish he knew Eddie was working on—pirouettes of raspberry shells with crème fraiche or some such sweetly named concoction. He felt a flare of envy surge through him at the thought Eddie was creating such sweet treats. Another thing blotting that particular employee's copybook.

He shook his head in frustration as he shoved the gum to one side of his mouth. "No, nothing wrong. And if you keep sneaking in to sample Eddie's wares, you're going to get bloody fat." He disregarded Carmen's moue of hurt and carried on. "But does he have to look so damn happy all the time? I swear that man is the fucking reincarnation of the bluebird of happiness." He ran a hand over his own shortly cropped light brown hair in frustration then tugged at his neatly manicured beard.

Carmen shook her head. "Baby, then you must be the reincarnation of the raven of doom." She sniggered as he scowled even deeper. "Giddy, honey, chill out. Eddie loves his job; you should be pleased you have such an asset in your kitchen."

Gideon turned freezing eyes on her. "Firstly, don't call me Giddy. You know I hate it. Secondly, I'm well aware of what an asset I have in my kitchen, thank you. I employed him, remember?" Oh, he knew about Eddie's assets. Those green eyes, that piercing stare, those talented fingers that look like they would play havoc with his dick. He pushed *that* thought out of his mind. "But I don't need to see his face wreathed in merriment every time I look at him. It's bloody unnatural." He scowled. "And I heard he broke another plate this morning? Does that boy think we're made of bloody money?" He chewed frantically on his bland piece of tasteless gum. He wanted a damn cigarette but that wasn't going to happen.

Carmen sighed. "It was just one plate. And he's twenty-four, not a boy. I wish you'd stop calling him that. You're only four years older than him, old timer."

"Well, he looks like a kid. All long limbs and flailing arms and costing me a fortune when he knocks something off or drops it." Gideon's inner bitchiness at not being able to control his feelings for Eddie rushed to the surface.

"Jesus, have you not had any for a while? You're being a real prima donna, even for you. Give the man a break, will you?" Carmen sounded a little pissed off as she marched over to Eddie's side, probably to resume her tasting session, and Gideon knew he'd better back off. A truly riled Carmen was not someone he wanted right now. So he ignored her, glowered and left the kitchen behind to enter the main restaurant.

It seemed as if all was usual, running like a well-oiled machine, but it never hurt to make sure. As the owner he took great pride in making things happen. He'd rather be in the kitchen creating dishes but he knew *that* wasn't on the cards. He looked around, his mood even darker. It was seven o'clock on a chilly September night and the place was packed.

Sarah Townsend, his very capable front of house manager and his right hand as far as the running of Galileo's was concerned, smiled at him as she led a couple to their table. This restaurant in London's Soho district was Gideon's pride and joy. It was also his home, as he occupied the large, roomy two-bedroomed flat above the restaurant. He was proud of his almost penthouse-like abode, furnished with all the mod cons and able to be accessed from inside the restaurant. It also had a private entrance, just the way he liked it.

Galileo's was currently abuzz with patrons. Some sat enjoying cocktails and pints at the highly polished dark oak bar along one side of the restaurant. Others were seated in the table area, an opulent arena of red and bronze décor, heavy wooden tables and the ambience of the Renaissance era. To the left was the huge brass telescope he'd found at an antique store and had cost him almost the price of what he thought a black market kidney would fetch. Indeed, when he'd been told the price he'd thought someone had reached inside and ripped it out. But he'd paid the money because he really wanted it. And what Gideon wanted, Gideon tended to get.

The ceiling was speckled with stars and constellations, a beautiful cosmic frieze that a local artist, Rafael Montero, had done for him. One Gideon had been fucking at the time but who no longer graced his bed due to the fact that said bed had been the scene of Rafael's infidelity with a man Gideon didn't know—some young college student called Richard. Gideon had promptly given Rafael his marching orders. They may have only been together three months but he would never tolerate cheating.

Gideon was lucky that Rafael hadn't been back to try and claim his "masterpiece" out of spite; he could insist it was his creative inspiration and he wanted it back. He wouldn't have put it past his rather fiery Latin ex-lover to have snuck in and whitewashed the mural over.

He watched the tableau before him now—impeccably dressed waiters bearing wine buckets, plates of beautifully prepared food being whisked from the specially created serving area to tables. Customers chatted and relaxed, looking for the most part as if they enjoyed themselves. He breathed a deep satisfied sigh and relaxed.

For a whole twenty seconds.

A loud noise from the kitchen made Gideon turn in consternation and his temper, already short by lack of sleep due to the nightmares that plagued him, flared as he stormed back in.

Christ, has the kid broken something else because by God, if he has, it's coming out of his wages.

There was a shattered mess of porcelain on the floor, and a flustered Eddie knelt trying to clean it up with a dustpan and brush. Carmen stood dabbing at the front of her dress, trying to get what looked like tea out of it with a dish towel.

Gideon spat his gum into the nearby dustbin. "Tripp!" He bellowed. "What the fuck have you broken now? Tripp by name, Tripp by nature, is it?" He'd heard the good-natured ribbing in the kitchen from the other staff about poor Eddie's klutziness.

Eddie's face flushed scarlet, an unfortunate side effect of being a fair-skinned redhead. His freckles stood out deeper on his pink face and his sea green eyes held a look of dismay. The rest of the kitchen staff looked on in trepidation.

Gideon's head-chef, a large Jamaican man named Jerome Sawyer, moved toward him with purpose and Gideon took an instinctive step back. While the two men were both work colleagues and friends, Jerome's rather fierce glare didn't bode well for Gideon. He was distracted from Jerome's intentions by Eddie's continued rambling.

"I was just cleaning up, Mr. Kent," he stuttered. "There was a bit of a mishap with the beef stock bowl—"

Gideon scowled. "There seem to be a lot of those. You are a one-man demolition squad. I can't afford to have you keep breaking stuff—"

"Now see here, Gideon, it wasn't like that." Jerome towered over Gideon now, his large, sausage-like fingers resting on Eddie's shoulder. "I can't have you thinking it was his fault—"

Jerome's words were cut off as Carmen's firm fingers pinched the flesh of Gideon's right side and he yowled loudly in pain.

Jerome blinked at being rudely interrupted but looked fairly amused.

Eddie's eyes were wide as he gazed from one person to another. Gideon turned to stare at Carmen angrily. Her face was set, her eyes unfriendly.

"What the hell?" he exclaimed. "What was that for?"

"May I see you outside, please? Thanks, Jerome, but I'll take care of this one," she hissed and flounced out of the kitchen, no doubt headed to the small office which they'd agreed was their neutral territory to discuss things out of earshot of staff.

Gideon stared after her then turned to a still red-faced Eddie. Jerome had a large grin plastered over his beaming face.

"Could you clean that up, please?" Gideon demanded, and passed a haughty glare at Jerome, who winked at him.

Bastard. He knows I'm going to get my balls handed to me somehow.

"Yes, Mr Kent," Eddie sighed wearily and bent down to sweep bits of pottery into the bright red dustpan he held.

Gideon couldn't help noticing the tight curve of his arse as he did so and the swell of what looked like a real bubble butt beneath the loose black-and-white-checked catering trousers he wore.

What the hell? Now I'm ogling his backside in public? Jesus, this is too much. I need to get laid...quickly.

He averted his gaze and left then walked into his small but comfortable office on the other side of the kitchen.

Carmen glared at him as she stood with hands on hips, looking fairly miffed. "*I* was the one who knocked that bowl off the counter, Gideon Kent. Not Eddie. So if you're going to garnish anyone's wages you'd better make sure they're mine."

He huffed. "Fine. He can count it as a warning for the next time he *does* break something. It's always good to put the fear of God into the staff." His tone sounded defensive even to him.

Carmen's face softened. "Gideon, you can't keep doing this."

"Doing what?" But he knew.

"Honey, I know more than anyone how frustrated you are at not being able to cook, to be a chef like you were before. I get that. But if you keep harassing Eddie, one day he's going to leave. And that would be a shame because he's one of the best up and coming chefs there is. You know that or you wouldn't have taken him on. But you're being a damn bully to him."

Gideon's stomach tightened at Carmen's words and he felt the old familiar sense of loss, grief and disappointment take over. The kitchen had once been his domain until the tools he needed to perform there had been cruelly taken from him. It was where he should be right now, creating signature dishes and making people's taste buds soar. Instead he was stuck with being a manager and a host. While he enjoyed it, it wasn't where his passion lay.

"Carmen, you're stepping over that boss-employee line," he warned. "Is it my fault I want things to run smoothly?"

Carmen came over and placed her hand, with slightly scary long black fingernails, on his wrist. "You're pissed off because you can't cook and you're taking it out on Eddie because he has what you don't. And baby, there's not much you can do about that yet. You know I believe you'll get those senses back someday. And it would come sooner if you'd talk to someone about that night, tell them the whole story. You never say anything about what you went through to anyone. Not even me." She regarded him shrewdly. "Are you still having nightmares?"

Gideon stiffened. "It's my business. Not anyone else's."

Carmen sighed, her eyes compassionate. "Everybody needs someone to talk to."

He clamped his lips. He wasn't getting sucked into Carmen's ploy to get him to talk about that night, the night he'd rather forget.

She saw that and sighed sadly. "So for now, let Eddie do his job. And what I say to you I say as a friend, not as an employee, so the Gideon 'line' doesn't count."

Gideon's throat was dry and tight. "I see. So I'm simply an arsehole then? Thanks for that."

Carmen sighed. "You are so damn prickly." She kissed his cheek softly. "But you're still a good friend. I'm going to go check everything got cleaned up in the kitchen seeing as how it was my fault. You might want to apologise to Eddie later. Make things up for the future, just in case." With a knowing look she was gone. Gideon didn't even want to think about what her last words might have inferred.

He slumped down into the office chair and stared moodily at the chart for staff leave on the wall. The trouble was…she was right. Ever since the accident six months ago, when the fire in his old home had taken away his sense of smell and taste, left his housemate dead and Gideon injured, he'd been a miserable git whenever he went in the kitchen. The sense of loss at who he had been, an award-winning, much talked-about chef in the city, was sometimes too much to bear.

He rubbed his eyes tiredly and closed them, recalling that night with a sense of dread. The explosion next door due to a gas leak, the fire licking through his shattered lounge, which had shared a wall with the doomed kitchen. Luckily, he'd been thrown away from the blast, away from the flames, but had been pinned by a wooden beam, his skin blistering as the wood smouldered. Hugh had not been so fortunate and had borne the brunt of it. He had lain burning on the floor, as the smell and stench of his roasting flesh had invaded Gideon's nostrils.

He'd woken up in hospital to find he'd sustained second-degree burns to his left side. The injuries had left the skin along his hip and stomach a little thickened and sensitive, although he'd definitely been the lucky one. Hugh and the neighbour were dead. A couple of days later, as he recovered, Gideon had realised his sense of smell and taste had disappeared completely.

The doctors told him his loss of smell was psychological, a condition called anosmia. They'd attributed it to him trying to shut his mind off from the odour of his friend's burning flesh. They said it could come back at any time, that there was nothing physically wrong with him, no blows to the head, no damage to his brain.

He'd hated the clinical diagnosis of a condition that meant the loss of his soul.

The doctor had tried to explain it. "Smell counts toward a person's sense of taste, and the term, *ageusia*, is used to describe your inability to do so. Be patient. You could still get both senses back."

His *condition*. Words that struck terror into his heart, the reason that his whole damn world had fallen apart. Some people with the affliction could taste salt or sweet on their tongue but he wasn't one of them. Everyone had tried to get him to talk to therapists and psychologists but Gideon wasn't made that way. He'd never talked to anyone about the events of that night other than to give some general detail to the police and paramedics. It was his cross to bear, even the montages in his head that woke him, sweating and crying out, in the middle of the night.

"Because what fucking good is a chef who can't taste and smell, eh?" he muttered as he rolled a pen between his fingers. "I'll tell you. No damn good at all. If I can't do it properly, no point doing it in the first place. Just like smoking."

Gideon had been a fairly heavy smoker before the accident and had enjoyed it. Now that the pleasure of inhaling the smoky odour of a cigarette and the woodsy taste of it on his tongue had disappeared, he'd decided there was no point in doing it anymore. Like a martyr, he'd given it up. It had surprised him just how quickly he'd been able to stop—with the help of his gum.

He frowned, gave up on his pity party and lost himself in menus, bookings and details for his accountant. Finally he'd had enough. It was close to eleven p.m. and time to do the rounds to ensure everything was shut down for the night. There was a soft knock on the door and he looked up to see Eddie standing there diffidently, looking ready to leave, his blue wool beanie jammed over his thick red-gold hair, his slightly protuberant ears looking endearingly elf-like. A fleeting thought passed through Gideon's mind that he would make a great Legolas with his fine bone structure and dimpled chin.

Albeit with hair the colour of flames and thick enough to run a hand through, long enough on top to wind it around a fist and pull that luscious pink mouth down towards Gideon's—

And there the fuck I go again. God, get a grip.

Gideon groaned inwardly as he regarded Eddie with narrowed eyes, shoving all thought of sexy elves, blow jobs and a naked Eddie Tripp out of his crazy brain.

"Uhmm, Mr. Kent, before she went home earlier, Carmen said that you wanted to see me before I left?" Emerald green eyes stared into Gideon's. Eddie stood firm as he hitched his backpack tighter to his shoulder and met Gideon's gaze unflinchingly.

Gideon tapped the pen on the desk in nervousness at having Eddie so close. Not for the first time he wished he could smell him, see if the man's scent was sweat or cologne, or soap or sweet-scented sugar from the creations he made.

"She did, did she? She can be a really interfering biddy. And how many times have I told you to call me Gideon? Mr. Kent was my dad. And I don't see him here."

He bit his lip as his snark returned in Eddie's presence. It was as if his mouth had no other way to react when Eddie was near.

Eddie seemed to be suppressing a smile. "It's a little difficult to be on first-name terms with a man who's always growling at me," he said, faint amusement in his tone. "I thought perhaps I should keep it professional."

Oh, Eddie bites does he? Not such a whippersnapper after all. I quite like that. The idea of him biting is definitely something I'd like to pursue.

Gideon shifted in the chair, trying to stave off the erection forming in his jeans.

Christ, that would be all I need, physical evidence of how he turns me on. I don't even know if the man is gay or straight and he'd probably deck me. They say redheads have tempers, don't they?

"Yes, well, about that. I'm sorry I growled at you in the kitchen earlier. Carmen told me it was her fault, so…" Gideon shrugged.

Eddie was grinning now, a wide, easy look on him that made Gideon's heart race just a little bit and the dick in his pants harden even more. "Wow. An apology. Thanks, I'll take it." He set his backpack down on Gideon's desk and rummaged around like Mary Poppins, an endearing pout of his lips making Gideon think of that blow job again. "I have something here I wanted to give to you, if I can find the poxy thing—ah, there you are."

He took out what looked to be a bedraggled red napkin, which Gideon knew to be one of the restaurant's special orders, and handed the soiled item to Gideon, who reached out and took it. There was something encased in the napkin and Gideon unfolded it to reveal a delicate pastry covered in icing sugar. No doubt one of the ones Carmen had enjoyed sampling earlier.

He felt a twinge in his chest. "I hope you aren't going to ask me to smell or taste this, because you know I can't, right?" He hadn't meant there to be a sneer in his words but he heard it just the same.

Eddie nodded. "Yes, I know you can't smell it or taste it, we're all aware of that, but I wondered if you'd mind giving me your opinion on the texture. Is it light enough, too heavy, does it melt in the mouth, feel like soggy cardboard..." He shrugged. "I wondered if you'd tell me, that's all."

Gideon placed the pastry on the desk and re-commenced his pen calisthenics. "I suppose I can. Perhaps later."

Eddie's face darkened. "Thanks. I know you'll be honest at least." His tone was testy. He hefted his rucksack onto his shoulder. "Well, if that's all, I'd better be getting home. It's late and I've got a bit of a walk to the tube."

He turned to go and Gideon stood up. "Eddie?"

The younger man turned to face him. "Yes?"

"Have a safe journey home. See you tomorrow."

Eddie smiled that wide smile again, the one that caused Gideon's sleeping heart to slowly stir with wakefulness. "I will. See you then." He turned and left.

Gideon stood there for a while and then sighed. He adjusted himself to get more comfortable then picked the pastry up, removed the napkin and popped it into his mouth. There was no sensation of sweet, no sugary caress to his taste buds, no hint in his mouth of raspberry coulis. He couldn't smell the almonds that would be in the pastry. He'd seen Eddie's recipe in the kitchen. Nothing. He felt the old familiar angst and resentment rear its ugly head as he chewed. It *was* light, flaky and melted in the mouth. There was nothing wrong with the texture. It was perfect.

Gideon swallowed the morsel, his heart tinged with bitterness, then threw the napkin into the waste bin. He gathered up his jacket and went to find Sarah to tell her he'd lock up and she could get the hell home to her family.

Chapter 2

Eddie heaved his rucksack onto his lap as he sat in the squashed confines of the tube and gazed out into the darkened tunnel as the train sped its way home to Kennington, to the small three-bedroomed mid terrace he shared with housemates Leslie and Taylor. Nicknamed Gay Way by Leslie, due to the fact that three gay men lived there, it was cramped, dark and a little mouldy in places but it was home to him now. His childhood home of Diss in Norfolk where his parents still lived was now just a memory. Eddie had his independence, his own small room and he and his housemates came and went as they pleased.

Eddie was lost in thought when a hand squeezed his thigh. Startled, he looked into a pair of red-rimmed, rheumy blue eyes and winced at the sour breath coming his way from a very buff, older man seated next to him.

Great. A fucking pervert who likes hitting on young men.

"Lost in thought, hey?" the pervert murmured. "Now what could a gorgeous young thing like you be thinking about then?"

Eddie politely removed the man's groping hand from his leg and shifted his rucksack over his lap to better protect himself. He'd been in situations like this before and didn't really want any trouble.

"I think that's why they call them thoughts," he said gently. "Because they're quiet and private." He looked away, hoping that the man would get the message. But no, there was his hand again, moving even closer to his crotch. Eddie sighed and tried to move further away but the woman next to him scowled fiercely as he encroached on her territory. Eddie closed his eyes momentarily and thanked God he got off at the next stop.

"It's a shame you hide that lovely hair under a bloody beanie," the man said, his fingers tightening on Eddie's leg. "I'd love to feel it under my fingers while you blow me. How about it? Do you fancy going somewhere with me next stop?"

Eddie stood up swiftly and moved away. "Not one bit," he said politely. "Not interested." The man didn't look pleased but Eddie didn't give a damn.

Why the hell did men hit on him? He didn't think he was all that much of a flamer, not like Leslie, and he didn't broadcast the fact, especially at work. Yet he couldn't go anywhere without being accosted by dirty old men or young bucks who wanted to bend him over and fuck him into next week. It's the bloody hair, he thought gloomily as he waited for the train to stop. *My effing red hair and pale skin that's been the bane of my life. Makes me look like a girl.*

Of course the fact he wore it quite long on top didn't help but he was damned if he'd cut it off just to make himself look less "feminine."

No, Eddie would rather look more like the delectable Gideon Kent, all male and decidedly sexy. He had one helluva of a crush on his boss and had done since he started at Galileo's. Gideon might be a testy bastard but he was testosterone personified with those smoldering chocolate eyes and that neatly trimmed dark golden stubble around his chin and lip. Eddie often found himself wanting to brush his fingers over it then lick that full bottom lip until his boss's stubborn mouth gave way. And joy oh joy, the man was gay too, even if he was off the menu being Eddie's boss. Eddie didn't really think icing the cake in his own bakery was a good idea. That was a clear invitation to trouble.

Even if I do want to rip those form-fitting trousers off his gorgeous butt and slap it. Besides, he'd never be interested in me. He likes them all dark and moody.

Gideon's last rather loud argument with his very volatile Spanish lover had attested to that, and the staff had stood in wide-eyed amazement as Rafael had stormed out of Gideon's office one day a few weeks ago and not been seen since. They had already broken up but it appeared Rafael had been trying to get some money from Gideon. Last Eddie had heard through the scuttlebutt grapevine, Rafael had gone to Spain with a new lover. He hadn't wasted any time, Eddie mused.

The train screeched to a stop and Eddie clambered off and started to make his way home. It was only about a ten-minute walk and he rather enjoyed it. The night air was chill, being September, but it was crisp and refreshing. As he reached the house, climbed the two stairs to the front door and squinted under the dim porch light to see the keyhole to open the door, he heard a frightening screech from inside. He'd just stepped back when someone came barreling out, almost knocking him off the stairs.

The person gave a muttered "Crazy fucker," as he jostled Eddie and then something whipped past Eddie's head. He saw with resignation it was yet another poor telephone directory being lobbed, no doubt, by Leslie.

"Stay the fuck away from me, you double-timing, cock-sucking, arse-dribbling twat!" Leslie's high-pitched voice screamed the invective as Eddie entered the house and found Leslie in a strop, phone in hand, clacking around on high heels, tiny silk shorts and a tight tank top that said he'd just been clubbing. It was after midnight, which was still early in Leslie's world of late-night partying.

"Oh, thank God you're home, Ed," sobbed Leslie as his eyeliner ran down his cheeks in stripes reminiscent of a zebra.

The man would be mortified if he could see himself. Eddie hated being called Ed but he let Leslie get away with it when he was in this state, which had been fairly often in the three months they'd been housemates. Leslie was a very high-maintenance twenty-three-year-old drama queen.

Sighing, Eddie took out a hanky from his jeans pockets. Leslie hurled himself into his arms, and he patted him on the back as the hanky flapped like a peace flag.

"That motherfucking bastard had the gall to suck someone off at the club tonight after he promised me we were exclusive. I saw a text on his phone from the guy. He even gave him his number!" Leslie's body shook with sobs.

Eddie pulled Leslie away from him and dabbed his zebra stripes with his hanky. "It'll be fine, Leslie." No one called Leslie "Les." He would have a conniption bar none if that happened and would probably scratch eyes out with his pointy fingernails. "He was an arsehole who didn't deserve you. You'll find the right one, I promise. Now come on and I'll make you a cup of tea."

Eddie was bone tired and wanted nothing more than to get into bed but he needed to get his friend settled first. He led Leslie over to the couch and plonked him down. While Leslie sniveled into his hanky, Eddie went to the kitchen to put the kettle on. He wondered absently where his other housemate was. Taylor was a bit of an enigma, a man who kept his private life just that, and who worked in a music shop down the road. He was normally home by now and as very good at sorting out Leslie's meltdowns with his no-nonsense attitude and snarky wit. The two men were very close and sometimes

Eddie wondered why they weren't a couple. They suited each other. He'd asked Taylor one day and he'd laughed and said Leslie was beautiful but not for him. Not in that way anyway.

Eddie finished making tea and took it into the lounge. He stopped short when he saw Leslie curled up on the sofa fast asleep, looking like a decadent floozy in his heels and red-streaked black hair sprinkled with glitter. Dark, silky bangs hung down over sleeping eyes. Eddie slipped off the stilettos, gathered the blanket from the footstool and covered Leslie with it. He put the steaming tea down on the coffee table in case Leslie woke up and wanted it then wearily went to bed.

Chapter 3

The following morning the kitchen was abuzz when Gideon walked in at around eight, a little more refreshed than he'd been in a while. He'd actually slept through last night with no dreams about burning men. Though the wet dream he *had* experienced had been one he wouldn't mind repeating.

He grinned as he pottered about, making sure everything was okay for the staff meeting. This early morning between eight and eight-thirty was for all the kitchen staff to ensure that the preparation for business breakfasts they offered was all in hand. From nine-thirty onwards, it was the Eggs Benedict Brigade that flocked through the open doors, ready for an early morning caffeine and hollandaise sauce boost.

Eddie was working on one of the stainless steel island tables between the hob and ovens. Gideon couldn't help notice that he looked tired, with dark circles under his eyes. His thick hair was once again caught up in a net on top and the normally short-clipped sides and back were showing signs of soft curls. Gideon felt an overwhelming desire to reach out and see if he pulled it, if it would spring back like a slinky. He masterfully resisted the impulse and waved everyone to pay attention.

"Morning. We have the Sherlock Holmes Appreciation Society in this morning, all twenty of the buggers wanting a hearty meal before they wander down to ogle the film set for the new series. So please look sharp, let's make sure we plate the food up as quickly and possible and get it out there. You all know the drill and I've no doubt you'll all do a sterling job."

He was feeling magnanimous this morning after that rather raunchy dream featuring warm lips around his dick and a cascade of red hair across his groin. In the cold light of day, seeing the man he'd dreamed about, he felt like a pervert and he tried not to catch Eddie's glance as those green eyes appraised him carefully.

"If we do a good job with this lot, they'll more than likely make more bookings, and it's nice turnover for us. Not to mention one of the members has a contact in the film production crew for one of the big TV series and she's promised to try and get their business for us as well. We all know word of mouth is essential in this game."

There was a chorus of agreement and Gideon smiled warmly at his staff. "Right, you all know what to do. In the meantime, there are a few other things I need to talk you about."

The staff meeting went well and twenty minutes later Gideon was back in his office poring about some accounts his book keeper had sent him. He popped a piece of gum in his mouth as he perused them. The business was doing very well and he felt a swell of satisfaction. He was a lucky man to have the team he had. Galileo's reputation for good food, great ambience and excellent service was growing.

He sat back in his chair with a happy sigh. A loud sneeze from the door announced Carmen's arrival. Gideon glanced at his watch. Nine o'clock on the dot. Carmen was only due into work at nine-thirty but was always in early.

"Morning, boss. I see you got Jenna's accounts. They look good, don't they?" She ambled in and sat down in the office chair opposite Gideon. Black lace-up boots thumped onto his desk, followed by thin black legs in tights.

Gideon shook his head ruefully. "You are so damn disrespectful of a man's work place, you know that? I honestly don't want to look up your damn dress so cross your legs."

Carmen snickered. "Wasted on you, my considerable attributes." She crossed her legs to protect her modesty and raised one multi-pierced eyebrow at him. "You'd rather look down Eddie's drawers then?"

Gideon's stomach lurched. "What the hell? What's that supposed to mean?" He swallowed and fumbled with the papers on his desk arranging them into neat piles. His gum chewing got more energised.

Carmen snorted loudly. "Oh come on, I've seen you looking at him with those goo-goo eyes. You fancy him," she drawled slyly.

"Don't you fucking dare spread rumours like that around," Gideon hissed. "Christ, I don't even know if the man is gay—" his voice tailed off at Carmen's not-so-subtle wink and thumbs up in his direction. "Oh. Anyway, I do not have the bloody hots for him." He scowled as fiercely as he could. "How do you know he's gay anyway?"

Carmen flapped a hand. "I know one of his roommates, Leslie. We've met at a couple of gay clubs when I do my whole fag-hag thing with my friend Pete. And I've seen Eddie there too."

Gideon felt a flicker of jealousy. "Really? Which club is that?"

"Bon Appétit," Carmen said with a sly grin. "Why, you going to go down there later, see if you can find him? I can tell you Eddie can dance up a storm. He's got a lot of really good moves and the guys love him."

Gideon squashed the feelings rising inside at the thought of Eddie gyrating with the horny guys at the gay club. "Good for him," he muttered. "He can be as big a dancing queen as he likes on his own time."

Carmen tut-tutted.

Gideon thought testily it was just as well they'd been friends for the last ten years or else he might have to turn nasty.

"We're going down there tonight actually," she said cheerily. "There's this whole goth night going on and Eddie, Pete and me are heading down there all dressed up to party. It is Friday night, after all, and none of us are working in the morning. Why don't you join us? Eddie finishes his morning shift at twelve but we're meeting back here at seven tonight to get dressed. He's going to need some help getting into the outfit I have planned for him." She chuckled nastily. "He is going to be so screwed walking a city block with his new goth look." She leered. "Maybe even literally when the guys at the club get an eyeful of him."

Gideon was morbidly and desperately curious but refused to rise to the bait. "No, I won't be going, so you all go and have fun. Not my scene." He turned his studious attention to the papers on his desk and attempted to ignore Carmen and the comment about Eddie being screwed. The images his mind was conjuring up were not conducive to his sanity. He had a sick feeling in his stomach at the thought of other men eying Eddie out and perhaps getting to first base.

"Well, if you change your mind, I'm sure you'll still be here at seven tonight." Her tone grew concerned. "Gideon, you need to get out, have some fun. This restaurant is your life; hell, you even live here," she gestured vaguely above her head, "but you need to relax a little or you'll burn out. Let Sarah look after the place on her own occasionally. That's what you pay her to do and she's good at it.

Think about it, okay?" She stood up and walked out the door to her own small office next to Gideon's.

Gideon booted up his PC as he busied himself with running his business in the forlorn hope it would take Eddie Tripp off his mind.

*****

It was around seven o'clock when he made his way back from a quick meeting with Sarah and heard giggles and deep masculine laughter from Carmen's office. He'd thought about Carmen's words earlier and decided that perhaps he might have an early night and get upstairs by eight tonight. He wasn't going to Bon Appétit, not on a goth night—Gideon shivered at the thought—but he might start that DVD box set he had of *Game of Thrones*. A night in sounded like a plan. He had plenty in his kitchen to eat and he was sure he could knock up something nutritious if not tasty. He still cooked for himself as it was plain, simple food that didn't need much effort. Eating nowadays for him was a means to end and no longer any form of enjoyment.

He wandered over to Carmen's office, jacket slung over his arm, and stood at the door. He stopped dead, his heart beating like a pacemaker gone wrong and his dick instantly standing to attention at the scene before him. Eddie stood with his back to him, in black skin-tight leather trousers, and Gideon could hardly drag his eyes away. The leather fabric hugged a taut, round backside, clearly defined in its two parts and leaving little to the imagination. His feet were encased in high-heeled, studded boots that made his normal five-foot-five or -six height closer to eye level at Gideon's just over six-foot. Eddie wore a black, silky, skin-tight tank top, showing off well-defined arms and pecs that Gideon didn't even know he had. Eddie tended to wear loose tee shirts and baggy jeans most of the time.

This strongly muscled, very sexy figure was miles away from the Eddie that cooked in the kitchen.

Gideon felt faint.

Eddie's rich red hair was streaked with what looked like black boot polish and he had long gold hoop earrings in both ears. He looked like pure sin on legs and Gideon wanted to sin with him, oh so badly.

Neither Eddie nor Carmen noticed him standing there. Carmen was dressed as usual in her goth fare and she was focused on applying lipstick to Eddie's lips. He was looking distinctly uncomfortable and trying to talk but Carmen was shaking her head.

"Shut it Eddie! This is a very delicate operation. God, you have great lips. I wish mine were like yours," she said enviously. "Yours are all lovely and full and mine are so damned thin."

Gideon had definitely noticed Eddie's almost bee-stung lips with their rich pink hue and lickable appeal before. They haunted his waking dreams.

"Urghh, Carmen, my balls are hurting," Eddie managed to gasp out as he wiggled a bit and tried valiantly to adjust his tight pants. "And my crack is chafing."

Gideon's own balls were hurting at the thought of what lay beneath Eddie's second skin and how he might partake of their particular charms.

"Slave to fashion, darling," Carmen drawled. "You look fucking fantastic and believe me, this outfit is going to get you so fucked." Her voice broke off as she noticed Gideon salivating at the door. "Gideon, doesn't Eddie look fabulous? Leslie chose this outfit for him, and boy, I have to say the man has a good eye. Just as well he's in fashion."

She pulled Eddie around unceremoniously so he faced Gideon. Gideon nearly passed out again from the rush of his entire blood supply to his dick. Eddie was wearing mascara and eye liner, his green eyes amazingly vivid. The black lipstick made his lips poutier and fuller. Gideon wanted to plunge his mouth down on that sensuous mouth and take it until neither of them could breathe. His dick was hard steel and his eyes were drawn to the clearly defined package that was Eddie's obviously very substantial cock. Gideon moved his jacket in front of him to shield the rabid beast that lurked in his chinos.

Eddie's eyes widened as his skin turned from creamy magnolia to blush rose pink and he stared at Gideon like a deer in headlights. If he could have bolted, Gideon thought he might have done so. However it was safe to say Eddie wouldn't be running anywhere in that outfit. With an effort he dragged his eyes back up to meet Eddie's gaze. Gideon swallowed.

Christ, he just noticed I had an instant boner for him.

"Well, say something," Carmen said in irritation. "Isn't he gorgeous? He is so going to pull tonight."

Finally Gideon found his voice. "He looks very nice." He winced at that statement.

Way to go, Gideon. The guy looks like your personal wet dream and all you can say is nice.

"He smells good too. Our Eddie has a man crush on Adam Levine and he's wearing his signature scent. Very woodsy and spicy. Delicious."

Carmen had a habit of describing smells to Gideon. It had taken some getting used to and he appreciated it most of the time but at this point, he was desperate to smell Eddie, taste Eddie, kiss Eddie, hear Eddie groan his name and rip those tight trousers off and fuck Eddie, and Gideon's remaining three senses were on high alert. He was sure that they had amplified since losing his others.

He got his one wish to hear Eddie, but not in the way he really wanted: *Panting and groaning in ecstasy as I plough him into the mattress.*

"Mr. Kent, I hope you don't mind us doing this here, but there was no way I could have gotten into these damn trousers without help and these boots take some getting used to. I'm not used to wearing heels and Leslie didn't bloody tell me that these trousers would be so effing tight and honestly, I can hardly breathe. I think my bollocks have separated." He ran out of steam and passed a hand over his hair, transferring some of the black goo to his hand. He looked at it helplessly and Carmen clucked like a mother hen. Gideon was speechless. Now he couldn't stop thinking about Eddie's bollocks.

"Here you go." She passed Eddie a couple of tissues. "Wipe it off, that stuff stains if you get it anywhere. Then I think, my gorgeous goth guy, that we're ready to go. Shall I call a taxi to get there or can you walk on those heels?"

Eddie looked down dubiously at his boots. "It's only a block. I think I'll manage as long as I can hang onto you. Thank God this is the West End and no one will look at me twice. Well, not that much anyway." His face fell. "Shit, where am I going to put my wallet? I'm always getting carded because people don't think I'm old enough and in these pants there is just no space to even slip a playing card." His pale freckled face glowered darkly as he bit his bottom lip with slightly crooked white teeth and Gideon thought he'd died and gone to heaven to meet a sinfully alluring angel.

Carmen picked up her small bag and slung it across her shoulder. "No worries, I'll pop it in my bag." Gideon thought faintly that her bag was hardly big enough to stuff a flattened dormouse in but somehow she managed to get Eddie's wallet in.

She grinned. "There we go. All ready to party. I hope you have plenty of condoms with you, Eddie." Eddie huffed as his skin went an even deeper shade of pink. Carmen raised an eyebrow in Gideon's direction. "Sure you don't want to come with us?" Her knowing glance made Gideon push his jacket closer to his traitorous dick.

"No, I'm going to watch *Game of Thrones*." No sooner were the words out than Gideon was mortified.

Way to confirm you are one sad motherfucker with no life. And bloody condoms?

His jealousy rose like a Mexican Wave at the thought of anyone else doing his sexy sous-chef.

Eddie's eyes brightened and he moved toward Gideon, tottering slightly on his heels. "*Game of Thrones*? Which season?"

"Season three. I've finished watching the others already."

Eddie's face fell. "I'd love to watch those. I haven't seen any of them yet and I do want to." He smiled that wide smile. "I have a bit of a thing for Jaime Lannister. He's so damn sexy."

The words were out before Gideon could take them back. "Well, you'll have to come up sometime and watch them with me. And call me Gideon for God's sake. Enough already with the Mr. Kent."

The breath seemed to leave Eddie's body and he regarded Gideon with a little trepidation and a definite hint of interest. "Err, yeah. Sure. We can do that sometime."

Gideon didn't miss Carmen's grin and she turned to pick up her wrap from the back of her chair.

"Well, now you two have a date, I have my own waiting for me. Come on, Eddie, let's go. Pete and Andy are waiting for us. We're going to have a few drinks at the bar across the street before the party."

"It's not a bloody date," Gideon growled. "It's just watching TV."

"You tell yourself that, boss man." Carmen said airily.

Eddie was still staring at Gideon, his gaze heated. Gideon held his breath as green eyes appraised him with needful intent. Then Carmen punched Eddie on the arm impatiently and the spell was broken.

Eddie blinked and yowled. "Ouch! Yes, by all means let's get off and see if Goth Boy here can make it in these bloody shoes." He stared at Carmen. "And just so you know—any future testicle damage I am billing to you personally." He winked at Gideon and tottered out of the room.

Carmen swished by and patted Gideon on the cheek. "Well done. See, that wasn't so bad, was it?" She gave a throaty chuckle. "What has that jacket ever done to you to deserve that death grip? Are we perhaps having a *hard time*?"

With a cackle of laughter, she left the room leaving Gideon in a state of tumescence he couldn't ever recall experiencing before. He could almost hear the shower beckoning so he could ease his aching dick.

Chapter 4

Two days later and Gideon was still avoiding Eddie. Yes, he'd been in the kitchen to check up on things, managed a few words to Eddie, but Gideon was doing his damndest to try and stay out of his way. The vision of him in his leather trousers and eyeliner still acted as Gideon's aphrodisiac to jerk off to each night, sometimes more than once a day. Eddie's name had become his mantra to regular orgasms and Gideon's hand around his own dick as he stroked and man-handled himself to imagined sounds of Eddie's breathy voice urging Gideon to fuck him harder.

With that in mind, it was very difficult to meet Eddie's eyes and carry on a normal conversation. In truth, Gideon had no idea how he was going to get over this obsession he had. So he tried to ignore it like any man would, hoping the urges would disappear.

It hadn't helped Carmen telling him all about that night and how every man in the nightclub had tried to pick Eddie up. She'd said airily that he had disappeared at one time for a while and she thought he might have got his rocks off with someone. Gideon had the impression she was trying to make him jealous. Worse thing was, it was working. The thought of anyone touching *his* Eddie made Gideon's blood boil.

Gideon muttered loudly as he attempted to un-jam the ancient printer in his office. His patience was at low ebb today after another night of nightmares and very little sleep, and his eyes were sore and gritty from being up since three a.m. He'd tried to huddle with a blanket on the couch and watch crap on telly but nothing had worked, and at five, he'd taken a shower and come down to his office. It was now ten and he was grumpy and irritated. His jaw hurt from chewing so much gum. He really wanted to smoke but knew he wouldn't.

The paper he was trying to get out finally ripped loose and Gideon swore loudly as it tore, leaving half of it in the machine.

"Fucking-arsehole-goddamn-printer," he cursed as he thumped it, causing the paper tray to jump off and hit the floor. "Why do I have to struggle like this?"

"Would you like some help?" An amused voice behind him interrupted his tirade and Gideon's heart leapt like a paper clip being sprung. He turned to see the grinning face of Eddie at the door, in his chef whites, holding a brown paper bag.

"It's fucking stuck," Gideon grumbled. Eddie moved into the office and shooed Gideon away from the recalcitrant office equipment.

"It doesn't help if you swear at it and hit it," he murmured gently. "Sometimes gentle works best." He put his paper bag on the desk and Gideon huffed and watched as Eddie's long fingers nimbly manoeuvred the printer parts around. Finally he gave a soft cry of triumph as a tatty piece of paper was extricated from its bowels.

"Eureka! There you go. All better now." His eyes met Gideon's. "It's pretty old, that thing, isn't it?"

Gideon looked down at the paper in his hand. "Stop being so bloody condescending," he said snarkily. "I would have sorted it eventually."

"Yes, but would the printer have survived the battle?" Eddie's eyes glinted with merriment. "I think it might have come off second best the way you were treating it." He turned back to the machine, checked the paper, pushed a few buttons and Gideon's Chamber of Commerce invitation to their annual banquet slid smoothly out and landed on the floor.

Eddie grinned, picked it up and put the paper tray back into place. "Party time?" He enquired with a wicked smile as he looked at the invite. "*You* at a boring Chamber of Commerce dinner? The mind boggles."

Gideon remembered that he wasn't really talking to Eddie and plucked the invitation out of his hands. "Was there a reason you were in here in my office?" He enquired. "Not that I'm not thankful you fixed that thing," he waved a hand at the printer, "But shouldn't you be in my kitchen cooking?"

Eddie's eyes narrowed. "Wow. Way to put me in my place," he said sarcastically. He picked up the brown bag. "Carmen said you were here at sparrow's fart and probably hadn't eaten. I made you a bacon sandwich."

Gideon was nonplussed. No one had ever brown-bagged a bacon sarnie for him before. "Oh. Thanks. You didn't have to do that."

"No, I didn't," Eddie agreed. "But there you have it. One sandwich."

Gideon nodded and went to sit down behind his desk. His dick was being most uncooperative and seeking attention and he wanted to hide the evidence.

Eddie gave a long-suffering sigh. "How is your *Game of Thrones* marathon coming on? Still watching?"

Gideon remembered with a pang that he'd extended an invite to Eddie the night of his goth party to watch episodes with him. "Oh, yes, still good." He looked up at Eddie. "Uhm, I know I said you should come and watch them with me but you do know that wouldn't really be a good idea if we, you know…" His voice trailed off as Eddie's eyes filled with something that looked like hurt. They darkened as he looked down at the ground then looked up.

"Sure, I know you were just saying that. It doesn't matter." His voice was even but Gideon heard the tremble in it. "I understand the whole 'employer-employee line that can't be crossed' thing." He turned and walked toward the door. "Enjoy the sandwich." Eddie disappeared, leaving Gideon feeling like he'd just kicked a puppy then thrown ice water over it for good measure.

But it isn't a good idea, is it? He's an employee and things could get awkward. It was the right thing to do. No matter how much I want him. He's too bloody tempting and I get the feeling he could see into my soul if he wanted to. I can't have that.

Gideon wondered then why he felt so damn miserable.

*****

The kitchen was very busy that night and Eddie had no time to ponder the fact that Gideon hadn't really wanted him to sit and watch films with him. When Gideon had first said that to him, Eddie had told the little warning voice in his head—the one that said employer/employee hook up was a bad idea—to bugger off and leave him be. It wasn't every day a guy got an opportunity like that.

Now though, Eddie felt rather stupid. He'd hoped it had been a genuine invitation and he'd subtly brought the subject up to remind Gideon. Well, now he knew it had all been nothing more than a throw-away comment. Eddie knew Carmen was trying to match-make and to be honest, he hadn't stopped her. If it got him where he wanted to be, i.e. in Gideon's pants, or Gideon in his pants, then he'd have been a happy bunny. Once again though, Eddie had read the signs wrong. He had a penchant for that in his relationships. Reading too much into them then getting his heart broken when he was left alone once again. For a while he'd sworn off dating and men completely but that had proven too much for his libido to handle. He wasn't really a one-night stand man and frantic encounters in bathrooms and cars were not for him. He needed some emotional attachment to have sex with someone.

He sighed deeply as he chopped parsley for his famous pan-seared trout in hazelnut butter. There'd even been a rumour that one of the food critics were here tonight "in mufti" so Eddie wanted to make sure he did his best.

Around him the kitchen was awash with noise, the sounds of cooking food, shouts and jokes, dirty one-liners and pots and pans clanking as the pot washers loaded the industrial dishwashers. Normally Eddie felt a real part of the kitchen but tonight, his heart just wasn't in it. He longed for the next half hour to go quickly so the kitchen would close and he could clean up and get home. He wanted to check on Leslie too, and perhaps share a beer with Taylor.

One of the other chefs, Andrew, nudged his shoulder as he stood plating up food. "Hey, Eddie, what's up? You're very quiet tonight." Andrew was about thirty, happily married with two kids and a willing part of the chef clique. He'd only been at the restaurant about two weeks.

"Oh, just thinking about the story that Max Warrington was supposed to be here tonight." Eddie picked up chopped herbs and sprinkled it onto the plate of trout. "One of the other foodies that was in the other night told Sarah about it; I think he fancies our Sarah but he's got no chance, her being married and all. Do you think Max is here?"

Andrew shrugged. "Who knows? Anyway, if he gets your trout dish and that incredible ginger soufflé you make as dessert, we'll have no worries. Your cooking is awesome, Eddie. He can't find fault with it." He smiled cheekily at Eddie, who placed the dinner onto the conveyor belt out to the serving area.

Eddie felt warmth flush his body at the compliment. "Thanks Andy. I'm glad you think so."

"Yeah, pity the boss can't taste it though. The poor guy must be really gutted at not being able to cook anymore because of his condition. I mean, he was one of the top guys in the city, wasn't he?

Won all those awards for his food and all. Now he's just the manager. It must really cut him up."

The one thing Eddie had learnt about Andrew in their time cooking together was that he was like a freight train. Unstoppable. Eddie tried to tell him not to talk about Gideon's condition as it was a bit of a sore subject and fairly private, but he couldn't get a word in edgeways as Andrew rambled on.

"You're the next gastro star, aren't you? I saw a piece recently in the local rag enthusing about your smoked salmon coronets and the guy said you were the next young rising chef to hit the scene, maybe even better than the boss. It even said you'd been made an offer by The Next Best Thing to go and chef for them? I bet there was a lot more money involved in that offer than this place, given that it's Michelin-starred. What are you still doing here then?"

Throughout Andrew's rather loud verbal diarrhoea Eddie hadn't noticed that the kitchen had grown very quiet. He felt a presence behind him and turned to see a dark-faced Gideon glowering at them both. The other staff were staring down at their work stations, trying to avoid being singed by the eruption they thought was no doubt coming.

"Mr. Calloway. Mr Tripp. Do you think the two of you could stop gossiping long enough to do the job you're paid for?" His tone was biting. Eyes almost black glittered with anger and Eddie saw a side to Gideon he'd never seen before. "We have customers waiting, and by my reckoning this kitchen doesn't close for another half an hour."

Andrew was pale, his mouth gaping open with dismay and Eddie thought he probably didn't look any better. He hadn't been able to say a word while Andrew rattled on and now felt a slow-burning temper at Gideon's obvious inclination to think the worst of him, too.

Gideon's glare at him stabbed like a laser beam. "Mr. Tripp, if you feel your talents are better suited elsewhere then please don't let me stop you. I'm quite sure I'd manage to replace you like that." He snapped his fingers and Eddie's fuse burned shorter at that dismissive gesture as Gideon sneered at him. "Please, far be it from me to stand in the way of the next rising young chef on the scene."

There was a collective gasp at Gideon's words as he turned and stormed out of the kitchen. For a few seconds the kitchen was silent. Then there was a complete outburst among the staff.

"Fuck me, I have never seen him that mad," Joao, the diminutive Filipino pot-washer was aghast.

"He was really pissed, wasn't he?" Jerome rubbed flour-coated fingers across his glistening sweaty forehead, leaving a light dusting against his dark face. "I'll have a word with him later, saying you were both doing your jobs, just having a natter. But Andy, you should really have kept your mouth shut about the boss's affliction. You know he doesn't like it being discussed among the staff. It's my fault. I should have stopped you." His tone was a soft warning to Andy and one of censure for himself.

He rolled his eyes at Eddie as if acknowledging it wouldn't have been easy stopping the express train that was Andrew, but it should have been attempted.

Andrew was speechless for once, but Eddie knew the damage was done. His throat was choked with disappointment at Gideon getting on the defensive like that without knowing the full story.

"Jerome, don't worry. You trying to defend us will just piss him off more when he's in one of his moods. It'll all blow over." Eddie loved working with Jerome. He was an institution in the kitchen, having been there for over two years. He was warm, funny and not at all like the Gordon Ramsey bossy-chef persona that television cooking series were so fond of portraying.

"Yes, but he was really mad at you and I'm not having that," Jerome said amiably. "You turned down that bloody job at the fancy restaurant because you like it here and he needs to know that. He's a good man. He'll accept he was in the wrong."

Privately Eddie thought that might be a pipe dream. Whatever bug was up Gideon's arse concerning him, it needed to come out. He nodded at Jerome. "It would be better coming from me. I'll have a word and set things straight with him later, if that's okay? Please, Jerome. Let me handle this."

Jerome sighed deeply then nodded. "But if it all goes pear shaped, I *will* talk to him," he warned.

Eddie accepted that but felt relieved. The last thing he wanted was for Jerome to get into trouble on his behalf. He looked around the kitchen. "Now come on, we'd better all get our arses into gear before he has another hissy fit."

Everyone got back to what they'd been doing before Hurricane Gideon had hit the kitchen. Eddie worked on autopilot, a sour taste in his mouth and his gut churning at Gideon's rudeness.

Chapter 5

Gideon blasted his way into his office like a mini tornado and slammed the door. His hands were trembling and he clenched them at his sides as he paced his office.

Fucking twats! How dare they get off talking about me behind my back! Just a manager, he said. I'll show him just a bloody manager when I fire his arse.

Gideon reached into his desk drawer and took out a quarter-full bottle of Jack Daniels. He opened it and slugged a mouthful.

And Eddie. I thought he was better than that. And what was the business about another job offer? I didn't know about that. If it was that damn good, why didn't he take it? Put me out of my misery seeing him here each day, untouchable when I want him so much.

Although in hindsight, Gideon couldn't recall Eddie actually saying anything while Andrew had mouthed off. He'd been too busy chopping up parsley. Gideon felt a twinge of guilt. He took another few slugs from the bottle and sat down in his high-backed chair, closing his eyes and running a hand over his chin.

Christ, Andrew's words had hurt. Hearing someone actually say it like it was cut him to his core. His future had been destroyed by a quirk of fate that in his eyes had left him less than the man he'd been. The overwhelming desire he'd had to become a "someone," a top-class chef, even more than what he'd been, had all been plucked from him in one foul spark of a faulty gas oven.

Guilt and shame stabbed him again, deeper and more painful. His housemate Hugh, a man he'd only known three weeks, had lost his life in that explosion, as had the woman next door.

I'm a compete prat. I am a fucking selfish bastard. At least I'm alive, even with some scars inside.

He gulped more of the JD, feeling the warmth flood his veins and the familiar buzz start. It was the only way he knew that he was actually imbibing alcohol. Gideon had a plan. Get absolutely shit faced and hopefully fall asleep down here and not have the nightmares.

*****

Gideon was woken by a low muttering and some really creative swearing. Finding his head resting cheek-down on his desk, he opened his eyes to peer blearily at a very shapely rear end at eye level at his side, perched on his desk. Said rear end was familiar and the voice was too.

"Bloody arsehole, stupid, self-pitying cretin, miserable excuse of a skin."

Gideon snorted slightly at that last comment, finding it funny in his drunkenness. He reached out and ran his hand over one firm arse cheek, squeezing it tightly through the jeans. The figure stilled and then stood up and turned slowly. Gideon grimaced as he gazed into flinty green eyes.

"Oh. So you're awake then? I've been trying to wake you up for five minutes, you idiot." Eddie frowned. "I told Sarah to go home; I'd take care of you. But you wouldn't open your bloody eyes. I was about to call Carmen and get her to come out here. Thought perhaps she'd have better luck rousing you." He glared at Gideon. "Would you grope Carmen like you did me?"

Gideon raised his head from the desk where it had been resting and shook his head. His brain exploded and he moaned softly. "Not Carmen. Too much trouble. And you're much sexier than Carmen. Don't tell her that though."

Eddie's lips twitched. "You deserve Carmen's wrath." But to Gideon's relief, Eddie put the desk phone back on the hook. He harrumphed and crossed his arms across his chest. Gideon giggled.

"What the hell is so funny?" Eddie sounded pretty pissed off but Gideon was sure he saw the start of a smile.

"You look like one of those preppy guys who used to tell me off in chef school for not following the recipes. All stuck up and holier than thou."

Eddie pursed his lips. "Hmm. Well you need *someone* to tell you what a fool you've been. You finished whatever was in that bottle." He picked up the bottle on the desk and then put it down again. "I need to get you to bed so you can sleep this drunk fit off."

Gideon chuckled, his big head swimming but his little head stirring in his jeans. "Yes, please. That's the best offer I've had all night." He pushed his chair back and tried to stand up but got dizzy. Eddie moved forward and took his arm with a surprisingly strong grip.

"Hold onto my arm and I'll help you upstairs."

Gideon clutched Eddie's arm as they stumbled out of the office and toward the back of the restaurant where the stairs to the flat were. He took advantage of the situation to feel Eddie up, grabbing at his waist, his shoulder, his arse, anywhere he could get traction. He even managed to brush the front of Eddie's groin once with the back of his hand, a gesture causing a sudden hiss from Eddie. Gideon was impressed by what he found there. The man was impressively hard.

He smirked seeing that even in his drunken state he could still give someone a hard-on. He himself didn't do well when he drank, so the swelling he had now pressing against his trousers was bound to disappear. He certainly wouldn't get to first base with Eddie tonight. But he might be able to steal a kiss.

Eddie got him up the small staircase and to his door. It was never locked so Gideon simply opened it and fell in. He stumbled and the room swam. Eddie clucked behind him and switched on the overhead light. Gideon winced at the brightness hitting his tired eyes.

Eddie looked around. "Where's your bedroom?"

Gideon flapped a hand in the vague direction of his room. Eddie helped him get there and then once inside, he steered Gideon to the bed then switched on the bedside light. He regarded him thoughtfully.

"Do you want me to help you undress or can you manage?" His voice was hesitant, his body language cautious. Gideon lay back on his comfy bed, his head on the pillows and waited for the room to stop circling in his brain. He closed his eyes and shut everything out.

"Just the shoes, maybe. The rest is fine." He cautiously cracked open one eye. "It's not the first time I've slept in my clothes."

Eddie nodded and sat on the bed, gently removing Gideon's shoes and then pulling his socks off. His feet twitched as Eddie's hands touched his bare skin. He'd always been ticklish there. His eyes flashed open and he saw Eddie's tongue move slightly to the side of his mouth as he focused on his task.

This feels good, having someone here taking care of me. Very nice. I could get used to this, could get used to him. God, I want that tongue in my mouth...

Eddie's eyes widened and he sat back, his breathing becoming deeper. Gideon had the sneaky feeling he'd said those last thoughts out loud from the look on Eddie's face.

"I want to kiss you." The words were out before he could even think about what he was saying.

Eddie shook his head. "Oh no. That isn't going to happen." He stood up and went to the windows, drawing the curtains and instantly making the room cosier.

"Why not?" Gideon was aggrieved. "Is there something wrong with me?"

Eddie snorted. "Oh, don't get me started on that one, sunshine. I'd be here all night."

Gideon's face fell. "Oh."

I can't blame him. Not after how I behaved today.

He reached out and caught Eddie's hand, holding it tightly and pulling him down onto the bed. Eddie hitched a breath as he plonked down and stared at him with wide eyes.

"Eddie, about what I said today. I'm sorry. I was out of line. It's your business what you do with your job. I had no right to say those things to you." His fingers slowly caressed the warm skin of Eddie's palm. It felt so right.

Eddie exhaled a deep gust of warm air that caressed Gideon's face. He supposed wryly that one of the benefits of not being able to smell anything was never having to experience anyone's bad breath. Although he wagered a bet that Eddie's breath was sweet, like his mouth would be.

Eddie shrugged. "It's all right. You were pissed by what Andy said about you. He shouldn't have really said that, that's your personal business." He watched as Gideon made slow circles on his palm with his thumb.

Gideon noticed his pupils were wide and dark. He chanced a long lingering caress up Eddie's wrist and felt the shiver run through his body. His dick swelled in spite of the drink and he stared at Eddie's mouth, visualising those pink, full lips around him, driving him crazy and making him blow into the sweet, warm cavern that was Eddie's mouth. Eddie was staring back at him, his chest heaving.

Despite his inebriated state, Gideon felt a sense of longing. His mouth ran away with him, his inhibitions at not wanting to get close to anyone disappearing like smoke.

"I wish I could smell you," he whispered longingly. Eddie's eyes darkened. "Smell your sweat and what makes *you*, you. Taste your skin."

Eddie stood up swiftly. "You're drunk and you don't know what you're saying," he said roughly. "I should go. Get some sleep." He turned to go.

Gideon sighed heavily as he closed his eyes. "It's the only way they stop sometimes," he whispered as his head swum. "The only way to forget what happened..." The world went black and he spiralled down thankfully into his darkness.

*****

Eddie watched as Gideon fell asleep. He was very confused and his chest was tight with both need and a little apprehension. The man lying on the bed, looking innocent and at the same time like a debauched satyr with his pink lips and long eyelashes resting against a tanned cheek, was an enigma.

One minute he's growling at me, the next he wants to kiss me, taste my skin? How much of that was him talking and how much was the booze?

Eddie sighed as he adjusted himself to try and get his cock under control. He hadn't missed all those sly touches to his body while he'd been helping Gideon up the stairs. The look in Gideon's eyes, a dark, desirous lust, had done nothing to quell the erection and breathlessness he'd felt at the man's roaming hands. If Eddie wasn't a gentleman, he'd be ripping the man's clothes off while he slept and satisfying himself. Instead, he draped the duvet over Gideon's sleeping form. No doubt in the morning he would remember nothing and if he did, he'd be as irritated as all hell that he'd come on to Eddie. It was the way the man seemed to work. Offer with one hand then take away with the other. Eddie wasn't about to make a fool of himself. He brushed Gideon's cheek gently with his hand and smiled in spite of his reservations when the man nuzzled into his palm with a faint, sleepy smile.

"What demons do you have?" Eddie whispered softly. "What makes you scared of sleeping?" Eddie knew the brief story, of course. That Gideon had been injured in a house fire, that his housemate had died and he had been left with no sense of smell or taste. It was one of the first things Carmen had explained when he started working at Galileo's as she put all the employment paperwork together. That and the stern reminder not to gossip about it or ask Gideon about it on pain of death. Even Carmen had seemed frustrated at the lack of knowledge of the events that surrounded that fateful night. It appeared the boss man liked to keep things to himself.

Eddie brushed a hand over Gideon's tousled blond hair. "Sleep well," he murmured. "Try to keep the bogey man out of your head." He turned and left the room, closing the door softly behind him. He padded down the stairs, made sure the alarm was armed before he left, having been given the code by Sarah, then exited into the street, pulling the glass doors closed behind him.

The street was still busy, despite it being just after midnight. This part of the city never slept. Theatre goers, late-night revellers, rent boys and those simply seeking company all milled around in dark corners, along brightly lit streets and alleyways. Eddie sighed again. He'd have to catch a late-night bus home as there were no tubes running. He hated buses with a passion but he didn't fancy the more than two-mile walk at this time of night. He didn't fancy it any time of the day actually.

It was almost one o'clock in the morning when he finally opened the front door to his home. Eddie thanked God he wasn't working today. It would give him plenty of time to catch up on sleep and also not to see Gideon after his drunken entreaty to kiss him. He tried to keep the noise down as he passed the small, darkened lounge and his heart leapt in fright when he heard a noise. Eddie laid his rucksack down on the floor and peered cautiously into the room. Someone sat in the large armchair, and Eddie swore they were talking to themselves. He listened, hardly breathing then heard a familiar voice.

"Taylor?" he whispered as he edged into the room. "Is that you?"

It was indeed Taylor, sitting stock-still in the chair, eyes open, a blank look on his face. His mouth whispered words that didn't make sense. Eddie saw his slim hands lying on his thighs, saw his shock of long, dark, curly black hair outlined in the sodium light of the street light outside. It was unnerving to say the least.

"Taylor?" Eddie swallowed as he moved closer. The other man gave no sign of recognition or acknowledgement, simply kept up the strange, stilted words he was speaking under his breath.

"Can't do this. Not going to make it." He stopped and Eddie edged closer. "It's not a fucking fairy tale. No gingerbread house here." His voice was strangled, as if it were coming from a long way away.

Eddie's skin prickled at the words. The words sounded familiar to him somehow but he was tired and he couldn't quite remember where he'd heard them before. Taylor continued his mumbling.

"Need to call Eddie. He'll know what to do." At hearing his name, Eddie moved faster toward Taylor. As he did so, his foot knocked the small side table and something fell with a loud clunk onto the wooden floor. In the dark recess and stillness of the room it was like a rocket going off. His heart beat fiercely and Taylor leapt to his feet, his hand to his chest as he stood up in fright.

"Who's there? Who is it?" The panic in his voice made Eddie reach out a soothing hand and clasp his shoulder which seemed to make Taylor even more jumpy as he stepped backward to fall into the chair with a soft exhalation of air.

"It's okay, Taylor. It's just me, Eddie."

Taylor reached out and switched on the overhead light. The bright light made both of them wince.

"Eddie, what the hell? Did you have to sneak up on me like that?" Taylor's usually soft tone sounded harsher than usual.

Eddie stared at him in confusion. "You were pretty zoned out there," he muttered. "I called your name and you didn't answer. You were, like, in your own little world."

"Oh." Taylor's words were flat. "I must have dozed off then." His café au lait skin coloured slightly.

Eddie shook his head. "You were talking to yourself. Not sleeping. What was all that about?"

Taylor stood up again, his face guarded. "Nothing. I must have been talking in my sleep. I do that sometimes." He tried to move past Eddie but Eddie placed a hand on his arm, stopping him.

"You were awake, your eyes were open. You mentioned my name. Something about asking me something, saying I'd know what to do?"

Taylor shrugged and Eddie saw the lie coming before it was even spoken. Taylor's dark brown eyes were very expressive, unable to hide much. He'd always said that was a legacy of his Mauritian mother and grandparents. "I have no idea. Like I said, I must have been dreaming." He looked at his watch. "You're home later than usual. Everything okay?"

Eddie knew he was trying to change the subject. He was exhausted so he let it go. He'd find out more tomorrow. "Yeah, had to put my crazy–arse, rat-faced boss to bed." He grinned. "He polished off too much JD and needed help getting home."

Taylor smiled slightly. "The crazy-arse boss you have the hots for?" His dark eyebrow quirked. "Did you manage to get him into bed then?"

Eddie chuckled. "Not in the way I'd hoped. I was a true gentleman and left him alone. You'd have been proud of my restraint."

Taylor grinned back, looking more relaxed now the focus wasn't on him. Eddie wondered what he was hiding.

Taylor nodded. "Well, it's late. I think we should both be getting to bed." His lips twisted in a wry smile. "Leslie got home about eleven, a little the worse for wear, but he seems to be over that other tosser that cheated on him. He brought another one home so we have an extra house guest tonight in case you see a stranger lurking about in his skivvies in the morning."

Eddie grimaced. "Thanks for the warning."

Taylor nodded again. "Anytime. Night, Eddie." He brushed past Eddie and left the lounge. Eddie heard the soft tread of footsteps up the carpeted stairs and reached out and switched off the light. Then he tiredly made his way upstairs to bed.

Chapter 6

Eddie was on his hands and knees on his bed, body bent low, one hand clenched in his sheets as someone pounded into him from behind. The incredible sensation of being filled so completely was coupled with a heady mix of animal need as the man above him drove his cock deep into Eddie's body. The scent of warm, sweaty man and the faint hint of some spicy aftershave drifted into Eddie's nostrils as he pushed back, urging the man to fuck him harder.

"You can do it," he gasped, as his arse was slapped by the man's balls, the sound welcoming among the gasps and groans of the man behind. "Christ, you feel good inside me. If I'd known it was going to be this good, I've have waylaid you sooner."

The gasping chuckle of Gideon Kent echoed in Eddie's ears as strong hands pulled Eddie's hips back and his lover sank deeper inside. Eddie moaned as Gideon leaned forward over his back and bit his earlobe, warm breath ghosting his cheek.

"You are such a slut," he whispered and Eddie's balls contracted up further, as he frantically fisted his cock with his free hand and felt the heat rise in his groin. "I love watching you jack yourself, you are so damn hot. I can smell your come, Eddie, and it smells like sweet release." Gideon's breath hitched and he gave a deep groan. "Hell, you make me feel like no one else ever has. When I say, 'come' you come, hear me? We try to do this together."

Eddie could only nod fervently as he felt Gideon tense, his strong thighs tightening as he pushed Eddie's legs further apart to drive deeper, and Eddie thought he might split in two as pleasurable as it was. The sound of Gideon's husky "Come for me," sent an eight-point-zero-sized earthquake tremor through Eddie's body. He cried out as his hand gave one last hearty pull on his aching hard-on and he released warm spunk onto the covers below him. Gideon gave a strangled cry and pulsed inside him, the warmth of semen coating Eddie's arse and thighs then Gideon collapsed on top of him, flattening him, still deep inside his now aching channel. He turned his face to find Gideon's mouth—hot, needy lips that sucked the life out of him and tried to choke him with a desperate tongue.

Eddie kissed back, wanting nothing more than this moment, this man in his body and his lips on his. Somewhere a bell rang and for a minute Eddie thought it might be the sound of his own passion translated to tinkling sleigh bells and fireworks like in the cartoon movies when two people kissed. He smiled at that thought then as the bell got more insistent and irritating, he turned to Gideon only to find he was no longer there. Eddie scowled and reached across to where the annoying bell sound was…

He woke from his dream upright, sweating, sticky with come and tangled in musty-smelling sheets that had seen their fair share of jack-off action lately and needed washing. His hand rested on his mobile phone as it trilled incessantly with his Big Ben alarm. He blinked owlishly for a minute, wondering where he was. As the dream faded, he fell back in a loose heap with a sense of loss.

"A fucking dream," he muttered to himself in irritation. "It was a dream. Definitely not the real thing, you horny twat." He looked down at his stomach and grimaced at the sight of it and his boxer shorts covered in white goo. His nostrils wrinkled at the rank, stale smell in the room and he clambered out of his bed, his legs boneless. He was still in post-orgasmic shock, as Leslie liked to call it.

Eddie glanced angrily at the phone that had awoken him from his sizzling sexcapade. He'd forgotten to turn the alarm off last night and the numerals stared up at him, the time of five a.m. in all their digital splendour imprinted in his head. He cursed and fumbled with the alarm to switch it off. He wrinkled his nose at the smell of himself and took a deep breath. Wow, that had been intense. He'd dreamed about men fucking him or him doing the fucking before but never with such vigour and not with Gideon Kent. This had been the wet dream to beat all others.

Eddie was what he called an "equal-opportunity man," not labelling himself as a top or a bottom but as one who rather gave into the moment and enjoyed whatever was offered. As long as both men got enjoyment out of what they were doing, who cared about labels?

He made his way out of the room to the communal bathroom to pee and clean himself up, clad still in his stained boxers and keeping a wary eye out for Leslie's houseguest—it might be five a.m. and he doubted anyone else would be up but he'd rather play it safe. He wondered idly if that would be what sex with Gideon would be like. He also mused whether he'd ever get the chance to find out. Eddie grinned to himself. If he ever got the chance to kiss the man or more, he thought he'd take it, consequences be damned. He could always go work for The Next Best Thing if Gideon fired him for sexual harassment. Now though, he thought he might just clean up a little, go back to bed as he had the day off and do it all again, only awake this time. That dream had given him enough masturbation material for a good long while.

*****

The man who had just featured so prominently in Eddie's wet dream sat shivering and naked on the ledge of his bedroom window, staring out into the early morning traffic below. His eyes were gritty, his head was throbbing and the cold sweat on his body from the early-morning nightmare he'd suffered still lingered. The drink had only deferred it, not taken it away. Gideon passed a trembling hand over his face.

Hell, I should never have drunk all that Jack last night. I'm a bloody idiot.

His gorge rose and he ran to the bathroom, just in time to hawk up bile and sour whiskey into the toilet bowl. He retched again until he was sure there was nothing left but his insides to come up. He leaned his face against the cool porcelain of the toilet bowl.

Pain. Burning pain that bit deep to the bone and made him gag. Smoke, stinging his eyes, suffocating him as the stench of cooking flesh insinuated itself slyly into his nostrils, a smell he knew he'd never forget. Desperation at being pinned beneath a smouldering wooden beam, heat hooking its greedy, invasive fingers into the side of his body, until he retched from the agony. A throat dry and burning that made him try swallow but finding no solace in his parched state. And finally, the shocking stillness of a friend as he lay dead no more than five feet away. Gideon would have wept tears of grief and despair had he any moisture left in his body to do so. Instead all he could do was lie there and watch a dead man burn and hope that it would all soon be over.

Gideon could still see Hugh's empty eye sockets staring at him from a burned, blistered face hardly recognisable as human. He shuddered as he remembered the flames licking at Hugh's body, and the memory of smelling the sickly smell of roasting flesh. He'd prayed Hugh was dead, even though common sense had told him he was, that no one could be burned like that without screaming. He'd been lucky in that the fire truck had not been far away and had reached the house within minutes of the explosion. The fire had been raging then and there'd been no hope for Hugh. Gideon remembered vomiting all over the firefighters after they'd freed him and loaded him onto a stretcher, while he babbled that he was sorry he hadn't been able to save his friend.

Gideon himself had healed well from his ordeal with minimal physical trauma, the skin on his left side from waist to hip simply sensitive from his burns. And while he could no longer smell anything, in some small way he was relieved, as reliving that smell of cooking human flesh might have driven him crazy. It was a double-edged sword, one he lived on the edge of every day. He wanted his senses back desperately, but he wasn't sure he could cope with them if he did regain them.

Gideon eased his aching body from where he sat hunched over the toilet, brushed his teeth then started the shower. Perhaps it might wake him up, make him feel better. He stood in the hot, steaming water of his power shower and a stray thought came to him as he soaped himself down. A vague memory of asking Eddie whether he could kiss him.

That made him groan in mortification.

"You stupid bastard, did you really ask him that?" he muttered to himself as he washed his balls, lingering a little on the thought of whether Eddie had accepted his request. He didn't think so; he thought he'd remember *that*. Eddie's wide, warm mouth beneath his, his tongue slicking against Gideon's, searching the deep recesses of Gideon's mouth, his breath hot and probably sweet from all the pastry tasting he did.

Gideon stroked his dick, softly at first then harder as he imagined running his hands over Eddie's taut chest, pinching the nipples until the man moaned for release. He pictured reaching down to cup the hardness at Eddie's groin then feeling velvety silk steel beneath his fingers. His breath caught as he imagined turning Eddie around as he jerked him off, then sliding his prick between those tight, round cheeks of Eddie's backside and sinking into delicious, smooth heat that would clench around him and drive him crazy.

Gideon closed his eyes and groaned as he tugged his dick harder, faster until he finally came, his semen washing down his stomach to the shower floor. He laid his forehead against the cool, wet walls of the shower and wondered what the hell he was doing.

At least that little sojourn into his fantasies had taken his mind off the nightmare.

Chapter 7

When Gideon arrived at work and found out that it was Eddie's day off, there was a sense of relief that he wouldn't have to face him mixed with a sense of ire that he wouldn't get to see him. Gideon wondered in exasperation when he'd become such a sad and needy arsehole. Sarah eyed him out with some concern when she saw him later that day. Her pretty face clouded over as he walked over to her in the dining area.

"Gideon, what the heck happened to you last night? It's not like you to pass out in your office, sweetie. Eddie was such a honey; he was so worried about you. That young man is a real treasure, you know." She laid a hand on his forehead. "You're a bit clammy. Is it just the booze or are you coming down with something?"

As much as Gideon loved Sarah, this maternal instinct she had for him made him feel uncomfortable. She was ten years older than he was and he'd not had to put up with it for a long time; his mother had died when he was only eleven years old and he hadn't seen his dad in years. Peter Kent travelled extensively as part of a geological survey team and the last time Gideon had seen him had been about four years ago. They'd spoken probably about eighteen months ago for five minutes. They'd tried to Skype and call more, but neither of them were particularly communicative– not that they made much effort.

Despite the headache, his throat still sore throat from retching and the nausea, Gideon smiled at her fondly. "It's just the booze. I was feeling a little down and decided to have a party by myself. Sorry you got involved. And yes, Eddie looked after me. He got me upstairs and into bed."

The knowing glance she sent him made him flush. "Not that way. God, between you and Carmen, there's no damn respite about your indecent curiosity about my sex life."

Sarah laughed, a lovely sound that always helped Gideon feel better. "I promise we're not matchmaking. But Carmen and I can't help seeing the looks you and Eddie give each other now and then. I don't think anyone else has noticed. It's just because we're such fans of you both." She stuck her tongue out at him and he grinned.

"Well, stop it anyway. You know he's staff and as the old saying goes, you don't shit on your own doorstep."

Sarah made a moue of distaste. "You can be so crude." She eyed him out. "When did you last get laid anyway?"

Gideon's mouth dropped open. "Jesus, Sarah, that's none of your business. I can't believe you asked me that." His face was warm and he cast a quick glance around him to check no one had heard.

Her laughter pealed around the rapidly filling restaurant. Patrons looked over at them curiously. "Well, since El Señor left, I haven't seen you serious about anyone. I suppose you're getting your rocks off somehow, maybe blow jobs in the alleyway and quick screws in your room after hours? Then you kick them out so no one sees them?"

Gideon swallowed. While she was right about his current sexual activity, there was no way he was telling her that. "Seriously, Sarah, you need to stop. This is *so* not a conversation I want to have with you." He turned and walked over to the tills to check on the employees and the registers. "Now perhaps you can make yourself useful and check on those bookings for tonight for that doctor's birthday. I think we're expecting a party of twenty and I'd like to make sure it's all sorted."

Sarah saluted him with a giggle. "Aye-aye, Captain, my Captain."

Gideon threw her a warning glance which only made her giggle more. He shook his head in amusement. He loved the two women in his life but oh boy, they were a handful. He sniggered. Well, Sarah was definitely more than a handful. Her husband had been known to espouse the delights of his wife's bosom, something that made Gideon fairly uncomfortable but that he accepted as the straight man's right. He felt the same about dicks. And arses. And smiling, full lips like Eddie Tripp's…

He gave himself a mental shake and went to work greeting patrons and showing them to their tables. It was a part of the job he enjoyed, chatting and meeting people. It took his mind off the fact that he should really be in the kitchen.

It was around eight p.m. when Michael Fortescue walked in. Gideon felt a sense of unease. He hadn't seen Michael since before the fire. They'd had a three-month relationship about eight months ago. Michael had been the one to break it off, citing he needed something "less prosaic" and to be honest, Gideon hadn't been that cut up about it. They'd had some sexual chemistry to begin with but not much else. Then Michael had tried to get back together when his last relationship had fizzled out and Gideon had said no. He wasn't a rebound catch. That conversation hadn't gone well and Michael had been bitter about it.

Gideon pushed the unease down deep and went over to greet him. He smiled at Michael and his partner, a young twenty-something with platinum blond hair, long lashes and dressed like a Calvin Klein model. Michael looked at Gideon with a faint sneer. He looked Gideon's attire up and down—his simple Burton Brothers suit of dark grey, with pale blue button-down shirt and striped dark green and navy tie.

Michael's lip curled. "Gideon. Good evening. I see your dress sense hasn't changed. Still playing it safe."

And that was the reason Gideon hadn't minded breaking up. Michael was a snob, a social climber. Gideon wasn't.

He smiled pleasantly at his customer. "Yes, I'm still as prosaic as ever. Can I show you and your companion to a table? Any preference? Over by the window or in the corner where you can be more private?"

Michael's pale blue eyes regarded him icily. "Somewhere quiet please. Daniel and I enjoy our privacy."

Gideon nodded and swept up two menus from the nearby table. "Very well. Follow me; I have just the spot."

The two men followed him over to a quiet, dimly lit section of Galileo's, to a table in an alcove, set for two, with fresh flowers and candles. Behind the alcove, people waited to be seated in the bar area. Gideon got them settled and handed them the menus.

"There you go, gentlemen. I shall have your waiter come over in about five minutes, give you time to check out the menu."

"You have a new chef, I believe," Michael said idly but Gideon didn't miss the glint in his eye. "I was so sorry to hear about your accident and your...*unfortunate* circumstances. That must be very difficult for you, not being able to cook anymore. From what I remember, it was a passion of yours." His hands smoothed the table cloth and Gideon wanted to brain him with the silver candle holder.

He took a deep breath. "Thank you. Yes, we have a couple of new chefs. I can guarantee the food will be excellent."

"I hear one of them, your sous-chef, is reputed to be even better than you were." Michael perused the menu idly but the edge in his voice was evident. "They say he's on his way to the top. Is he here tonight?"

Gideon willed his racing heart to calm down. "No, I'm afraid Eddie isn't working tonight. But Jerome is top of his game and I'm sure the food will be to your liking. Now if you'll excuse me, I need to check on something." Gideon noticed the confused glances Daniel was giving him and Michael and he felt a little sorry for him. He obviously didn't know he and Michael had a history.

Michael smiled at Daniel even as he addressed Gideon. "How does it work not being able to smell or taste anything? I can't imagine losing two of your senses like that. It must be quite a challenge. I'd hate it. So you can't smell my new Paco Rabanne fragrance then?" He waved his wrist in Gideon's direction. Gideon's nostrils flared instinctively but there was nothing. "And to go through what you did, with your friend burning to death—are you seeing someone for therapy? If not I can recommend someone if you like." His smile didn't reach his eyes.

Gideon felt a little dizzy as a panic attack threatened. He hadn't had one in months and now it was all getting a bit too much. He tried to take quick, deep breaths to stop the wooliness growing in his head.

"I'm fine, thank you Michael." His tone was sarcastic. "Gratified at your concern, seeing as how you didn't bother to contact me at all at the time. Anyway, I think you've had your say. I hope you both enjoy your meal." He nodded and saw Daniel frown and lean over and whisper to his companion as Gideon turned and walked back to his office. He took deep, cleansing breaths each step, but the tingling sensation in his fingers worsened, his mouth was dry and he was sweating. He needed to stave this off. He couldn't afford an attack now.

In his office he made it to his chair and sat down in it, the feeling of dread seeping through his bones and causing his hands to shake.

"Please, not now," he whispered. "Not now. Fight this, you weak bastard. Fight it."

"Gideon, here. Drink this." Gideon jumped as a glass of water was pressed into his hand. He took it and drank it numbly. Eddie stood there, his eyes shadowed, one warm hand slowly stroking Gideon's arms, calming him like a rider would calm a horse. That slow, tender caress centred him as he drank thirstily now and finished the water. He put it down on the desk and stared at Eddie.

"I didn't think you were working tonight," he said hoarsely. "What are you doing here?"

"I needed to drop something off for Andrew as it's his day off tomorrow. Some tickets for a show tomorrow night that I promised him. I can't make it so he took them." Eddie scowled. "I saw that prick talking to you and you didn't look too well. I heard most of what he said." He looked shame faced. "I wasn't spying, honest; I was in the alcove behind their table—"

Gideon waved a hand at him tiredly. "It doesn't matter. You're right—he is a prick." He was feeling more balanced now, Eddie's calming presence helping.

"And you're not a weak bastard," Eddie said fiercely. "From what I heard you went through hell and anyone would have a few issues."

Gideon loved the protectiveness emanating from that sexy body. It had been a long time since anyone had cared enough about him in that way.

Eddie stared at him worriedly. "I thought you looked agitated. My mum suffers from panic attacks; you had the same look."

Gideon snorted. "Thanks." There was an almost comfortable silence.

"Why couldn't you make your show?" Gideon asked Eddie softly.

Eddie looked embarrassed. "I have to help a friend. My roommate Leslie needs a plus one for an event he's going to, it's important to him. So I said I'd go with him."

Gideon's jealousy rose to the fore. "Are you and this friend—together—then?"

Eddie looked shocked. "Good God, no. Leslie is not a fuck buddy."

Gideon's dick rose at that comment. "So where are you going then?"

Eddie looked a little gloomy. "Some damned fashion show. Leslie is a trainee buyer for an independent fashion house and this is his chance to sparkle with the boss *and* say a huge Fuck You to his ex." He sighed. "I have to wear a tux and clean up nicely." He shrugged. "Not my ideal date but I'll get free food and help him out."

"You do that a lot," Gideon murmured. "Help people out. This is the third time you've come to my rescue. My knight in shining armour." He knew he was taking this down a route he really didn't want to go—*shouldn't* go—but he couldn't help it. Eddie was special.

"I like you," Eddie said simply. "Something tells me you could do with a bit of looking after."

Gideon felt the air shift and change around him, the sexual tension evident. It wasn't only his dick that was enjoying this. He really liked Eddie too.

"Are you feeling better then?" Eddie moved over to stand behind Gideon as he sat. Slowly, almost reverently, he began to rub Gideon's shoulders, his fingers digging into the knots and muscles. Gideon gave a soft moan and leaned back into his hands. It felt so good to have hands on him, to have somebody care about him. Eddie seemed to be a very tactile person.

Eddie hadn't finished talking. "Oh and by the way? That dickhead's Paco Rabanne fragrance? He obviously emptied the bottle on himself and it was all wrong for him. He smelt like a rancid kipper."

Gideon snorted with sudden laughter, his shoulders shaking with mirth at the dry words. He looked back to see Eddie looking down at him, a strange expression on his face. Before Gideon knew it, there was nothing but the closeness of Eddie's face and his mouth taking Gideon's in a deep, possessive, upside-down kiss, his tongue pushing its way into Gideon's mouth as the action targeted Gideon's needy dick to the point of pure hedonism. Gideon sighed into Eddie's mouth as he opened his own, his tongue finding Eddie's. That sweet mouth left his suddenly and Gideon groaned, needing more of it. Eddie swivelled the chair around and sat down, straddling Gideon, locking his fingers into Gideon's hair and taking his mouth again. Gideon thought he would burst from pleasure. His arms snaked out, gripping Eddie's arse and pulling them closer together.

Eddie was now sitting directly on his dick, those tight buttocks of his grinding against him and there was no way *that* could be continued right here, right now. Anyone could come into the office and find them dry humping each other. As much as Gideon wanted Eddie, this wasn't the right place. He managed to extract his swollen and bitten lips from Eddie's suction to make a feeble protest.

"Eddie, this isn't right. Anyone can come in and I don't want them to find us like this."

Eddie's eyes were black, his erection hard against Gideon's stomach, virtually pushing through the fabric of his jeans. He moved back to stare at Gideon through unfocused eyes. His lips were pink and wet and Gideon shivered with need.

God, he is so mine. I want him so badly. What the hell is this man doing to me?

"Okay. Where then?" Eddie said huskily and it went straight to Gideon's dick.

"Later, after everyone leaves. Come back to the restaurant before close up and go upstairs to my flat. I'll see you there when I'm done."

Eddie nodded then leaned forward and swiped his tongue sexily over Gideon's bottom lip. Gideon was already ready to explode. He pushed Eddie off his lap and stood up, breathing heavily.

"God, you are something else. If you touch me again I'll blow and I can't have that. Leave it for later. Think about what I'm going to do to you."

Fuck I hope he wants me inside him. But either way, he can have me.

"You want inside me, Gideon?" Eddie's voice was low, sensual. "I don't mind either way. Whatever you want."

The man is a mind reader as well as being the sexiest man on earth.

"Oh Jesus, Eddie. Please go." Gideon's voice wavered. "Let me finish up here and I'll see you later."

Green eyes blazed bright. "That you will." With one last, smouldering look at him, Eddie turned and walked out of the office. Gideon tried to calm his pulse down to just a potential heart attack instead of total brain annihilation. He didn't think he had any blood left to spare; it was all in his groin. Finally he managed to get his libido under control and took a tiny sip—well, a gulp—of the second bottle of JD he had in his drawer. It wasn't the brightest thing to do given his overindulgence last night, but he needed to calm down. In another few hours, he would be alone, in his room, with Eddie, both of them naked and horny and that alone was enough to induce another panic attack of a different kind.

Chapter 8

Eddie walked out of Galileo's in a state of complete meltdown. Not only had he just kissed his boss, he'd also promised to let him fuck him later. While this had been high on his list of "Things to Do with Gideon" he wasn't sure he was really ready for it.

"You are a horny bastard," he muttered to himself as he made his way home on the tube, his denim jacket placed strategically on his lap to conceal the problem rearing its literal head in his groin. Eddie felt rather confused actually. He'd never been as aggressively sexual before as he had been with Gideon earlier. Something in the man brought out his inner dominant beast and strangely enough, Gideon, a man he'd have imagined was a complete alpha male in the sack, had gone with the flow.

"Huh," he muttered as he sat on the tube as it wound itself around dirty corners and dimly lit concrete walls. "Who would have figured *that* of either of us?"

The woman across the aisle from him gave him a tentative smile as she juggled with various parcels on her ample lap. He nodded his head back at her. Mr. Perv, the man who had grabbed his leg the other day and asked him to go with him, sat two seats down. Eddie hunkered down, trying to make himself invisible. It didn't work. Mr. Perv caught his eye and stood up to come sit beside him. Eddie hadn't realised just how wide the man was. Of course it could have been the bulky suede jacket he wore. He looked like a damn wrestler. Eddie moved further away and studiously ignored him. The man licked his lips lasciviously and Eddie took out his iPhone and put in his earbuds. Irritation at being so dismissed emanated from the man but Eddie didn't give a fuck. He wanted to get home, beat off, relieve some of the tension he felt then go back for more later.

When he got off at his stop Mr. Perv did too. Eddie knew it wasn't his normal stop and he kept a wary eye on the man. He seemed harmless enough, following the same route but not too close. Eddie sighed.

I'm just being paranoid. The poor sod's probably just on his way to a friend or something. Maybe a local peep show. He grinned. With music blaring in his ears, he hummed softly to the tune as he made his way home in the darkness. The route was sparsely populated, and Eddie was nearly home.

He relaxed as the sight of the house came into view and was so wrapped up in his music that when something shoved him with great force into the nearby alley, he could only shout out in panic and turn to see who or what had pushed him. His head rocked sideways due to a violent slap across his cheek and his earbuds were pulled from his ears as his phone went slamming to the ground.

Mr. Perv stood before him, his face a mask of fury as he pushed Eddie back against the wall, pinning his arms to his sides. Eddie felt fear at that moment that he'd never experienced before. He was fairly scrappy when it came to a fight but he didn't think he stood a chance against this man. He remembered his father always telling him to stand up to bullies, get on the defensive so he gave it a try.

"What do you think you're doing, you arsehole?" he spat at the man as loud as he could. "Let me the fuck go, Gigantor." Eddie tried to bring his arms up but the man grinned nastily and pinned them above his head with one meaty, sweaty hand.

Shit, this guy was really strong.

Eddie's heart beat faster and he felt sick.

Mr. Perv smiled at him and it was a dreadful sight. "You're a cock tease," he whispered, rancid breath wafting into Eddie's face. "A little cocksucker, and that's exactly what you are going to do right now. And I'm going to make sure you don't get any clever ideas and use those teeth of yours while you're down there." He reached into the pocket of his bulky jacket with his free hand and drew out a switchblade which sprung to life with a glint of steel. "This will be in my hand while you suck me, little boy, and if I think for one minute that you are going to me harm, I will slice you like a chicken fillet." He gestured downward. "Now get on your knees, unzip me and do what little cocksuckers do best."

Eddie's body was frozen and his eyes darted around, desperately trying to find some help. His throat clenched and he looked into the implacable eyes of his captor, seeing no mercy. Mr. Perv released Eddie's hands and slowly, deliberately, he forced Eddie to his knees. His hand pushed down on Eddie's shoulder and Eddie bit his lip, trying to stop from crying out at the iron grip. He didn't want the man to have that satisfaction. Eddie pushed back, his hands trying to find a place to hit, to stop what was happening, but the man had at least ninety pounds on him. He landed one punch against the man's chest, but he winced when it seemed to hit steel.

His attacker laughed then punched Eddie on the side of his cheek, causing a ringing in his ears. The skin opened and his head spun. Through splitting pain, he tried feebly to hit back but his hand again hit the taut flesh of the man's stomach. Mr. Perv fumbled with his trousers and a large, purple cock sprung up in front of Eddie's face. It was pushed toward Eddie's mouth and he pressed his lips together.

He stared up at the man, whose lips were coated in spittle. The hand on his shoulder grew tighter as lust flared in his attacker's eyes.

Eddie snarled. "I am not putting that in my mouth, you fucker. You can slice me all you want." Brave words and Eddie just hoped that they wouldn't be his last. The knife wandered slowly down to his cheek and was drawn across the skin. Eddie hissed in pain as his skin parted and he felt the warmth of blood on his flesh. Now he was more scared despite his bravado.

"I have no problem marking you, boy," the voice above him growled. "Make you look not so pretty anymore." The knife made its way toward one of his eyes. Eddie swallowed and closed his eyes as Mr. Perv chuckled. "Maybe I should take one of these beautiful green marbles you have and keep it with me as a reminder that you sucked my cock? I can look at it when I jack off and remember what you used to look like." The tip of the knife was pressed into his eye and Eddie tried to draw his head back, away from the weapon.

Then all hell broke loose. A fearsome and unworldly shriek rent the air as something launched itself at Mr. Perv's back, knocking the blade from his hand to clatter on the pavement. A pale hand raised a sharp-heeled shoe with three inch stiletto heels, repeatedly slamming into Mr. Perv's head and face.

Eddie's attacker cried out in anger and shock and tried to rid of himself from what Eddie now saw was a spitting Leslie, all one hundred and twenty pounds of him, clinging to the man like a limpet and using a shoe as his weapon of choice.

"Get off me, you little wanker," Mr. Perv yelled as he tried to rid himself of his burden. "Stupid git, get off me!" He stumbled around in circles as he tried to pluck Leslie off his back, his trousers around his ankles.

"Motherfucking arsehole prick," Leslie screeched at the top of his voice as he wielded his shoe with malevolent intent. "Hurt my friend, you bastard? We'll show you. Taylor, I'm gonna get off then you smack him, baby. Right across the head." Leslie made a quick dismount off the man and landed gracefully on the street, black stockings under his tight shorts now the worse for wear and definitely laddered.

A thwack sound split the air and Eddie watched in amazement as his would-be molester fell face down onto the pavement. Eddie looked up to see a grim-faced Taylor holding what looked like a rubber truncheon.

"Eddie, are you okay?" Taylor said anxiously as Leslie danced around the fallen man with a cackle of glee. "Did we get here in time? You have blood on your face."

Taylor helped Eddie to his feet. Then he leaned over and checked the now supine man on the pavement. Eddie saw him heave a sigh of relief.

"He's breathing, just dazed. I'll keep an eye on him so he doesn't get up." He waved what Eddie could now see was definitely a truncheon. "I never thought I'd get the chance to hit someone with one of these. Pretty cool."

Eddie's mind was whirling. Leslie was fussing over him, clucking his tongue as he saw the cut on one of Eddie's cheeks and the split on the other.

Eddie winced. "I'm okay, Taylor. Just a little damaged. Arsehole didn't get what he wanted. But how the hell did you know I was here? Did you see me?" He looked wildly around, realising that there was no way he could be seen from across the street where the house was.

Leslie waved a manicured hand. "We were at home. Taylor just knew you were in trouble. Like the time I got really plastered and those guys were going to drag me down to that gang bang and he found me and got me home? Remember? Taylor said he had a feeling you needed help. He is so damn amazing." He glanced down at his legs and frowned. "Fuck, look at these damn stockings. They're bloody ruined." He kicked the man lying prone on the pavement. "They cost me twenty quid, you bastard!"

The wail of sirens split the air and Eddie's mouth gaped open. "You called the police?"

"Damn right we did, honey," Leslie crowed. "Just before we ran over here, Taylor dialled a mate of his on the force and told them we had a mugging in the alley."

The whole evening had become a little surreal to Eddie and he grabbed Taylor. His legs were shaking and seemed no longer capable of supporting him.

"I don't want you guys getting into trouble for me, maybe you should split—"

Taylor shook his head and gripped Eddie's arm. "No, we should be fine. I mean, Leslie whipped this guy's arse with a shoe, I got in a good smack, we'll say you did the same and he went down. There's three of us. And his cock is out and there's a knife that will have his prints all over it. I dare say the police will make the right connections and cart his sorry effing arse off to jail."

Eddie stared at him. Taylor looked like a force to be reckoned with as he stood there, his features set and a look of complete determination on his face. Eddie's legs gave way and he would have tumbled to the ground had Taylor and Leslie not been holding him up.

"Just hold out a little while longer," Taylor said softly. "Then we'll get you home and sort you out."

Eddie nodded gratefully. An hour and a half later, he was seated in the old, worn armchair in the small lounge, with a cup of chamomile tea pressed into his shaking hand by an insistent Leslie. He would have preferred a shot of brandy but Leslie had glowered at him and bit out something about chamomile being better than booze in this situation. Eddie had refused hospital treatment for his damaged face and instead Leslie had patched him up using the home first aid kit.

The police had come and gone, taken statements, carted the now fully conscious Mr. Perv off in handcuffs and told the three of them to be ready for more enquiries if needed. Leslie had simply explained that he'd been on his way home from a club night and seen what was happening. He'd called Taylor to come and help and bring his trusty truncheon. It had helped that Taylor had seemed to know one of the policemen, Sergeant Shaun Grant, who had arrived on the scene and been very supportive. He'd even given Taylor's hand a squeeze when he'd left. From the look in his eyes, he'd wanted to do more.

The truncheon had apparently been a gift from said Sgt Grant to Taylor as part of a self-defence class he'd undertaken. Once this had been explained and confirmed by the policeman, and Leslie had butted in and gone on and on about the virtues of the implement, being virtuous about the fact it was a better self-defence tool than a knife or a gun, the policeman had wearily agreed and taken it away as "evidence."

"So Taylor, how did you know I was in trouble?" Eddie sipped his tea under Leslie's gimlet eye and tried to keep his distaste at the dishwater taste from showing on his face. His cheek stung where it had split open and he swore his ear was still faintly ringing.

Taylor sat next to Leslie on the worn couch. He sighed and ran a hand over his curly dark hair and stretched his slim body as if he were tired. "I sense things. See them sometimes." He stopped as if he expected Leslie and Eddie to burst into disbelieving laughter. When they didn't he carried on. "My mother had it too. She could sense things, before they happened."

"Like premonitions?" Leslie said in awe, his big blue eyes wide. Eddie loved Leslie's deep blue eyes, fringed with sooty back lashes, and thought they were his best feature.

Taylor nodded. "Yeah, sort of. I've been able to do it since I was a kid." He cleared his throat uncomfortably. "I don't tell many people about it because they think I'm a freak. Or ask me if I can tell them the lotto numbers for a Friday night. It doesn't work that way. It's pretty random."

"Wow." Eddie was impressed. He was quite into that kind of thing anyway so hearing someone who could actually do cool stuff like this was quite a win for him. "So how do you see things, is it like a movie, does it play out in your head?"

Taylor shook his head. "No. I catch glimpses of stuff, images, just fleeting random things, and I feel things and just know. Like with you"—he waved at Leslie—"I saw these guys holding you between them, saying they were going to fuck you and just knew they were up to no good. I saw the club logo and that's when I came down and dragged you out." He scowled. "You shouldn't have been in that state anyway, Leslie. It's too easy to let people get to you when you're drunk like that."

Leslie had the grace to look abashed. "I know, baby. Normally I have someone watching my back when I get like that but he'd disappeared somewhere, probably for a quickie in the bathroom and I lost it for a minute."

Taylor nodded. "Well, you need to be more careful. Make sure you have me or Eddie here looking out for you next time. We won't let you down."

Leslie reached out and laid a soft hand on Taylor's arm. "Thanks, sweetie. I promise I'll be more careful."

"So what did you see about me then?" Eddie asked curiously.

Taylor shrugged. "I just felt—unsettled, I guess. I kept having this flashback of that alleyway and I knew it because I see it every day. I saw you on your knees," he stopped, looking grim, "And I didn't get the feeling it was voluntary. So I told Leslie about it and being the prima donna he is," he grinned at Leslie who grinned back, "He was on the phone calling 999 then running across here with me hot on his heels."

"You should have seen him, Eddie." Leslie shivered. "It was fucking spooky. He just stood there, all zoned out and kept saying, 'Eddie's in trouble.' His eyes were all blank like there was no one home. And he was pointing to the alley and saying shit like, 'He's over there, the guy's going to cut him.'" Leslie harrumphed. "Well, I just *had* to do something. He was *very* convincing."

Eddie grinned despite the chill running down his spine. "And if it had been a false alarm and Taylor was just messing with you or wrong?"

Leslie waved a hand. "Oh well, better safe than sorry I say. I could have made some excuse up to the boys in blue if there'd been nothing there. But as it turned out, you weren't wrong, were you, Tay?" He grinned. "Tay here is a regular old psychic."

"Is that what happened the other night?" Eddie asked quietly. "When I found you in here, all creeped out, talking about gingerbread and fairy tales?"

Taylor nodded. "Yeah. I didn't see that much of that, just had this feeling someone you knew was in trouble. But I don't remember much about it. Maybe it's sorted itself out." He sounded hopeful. "It normally only happens with people I'm close to, or have some kind of connection with."

"Gingerbread and fairy tales rings a bell somehow but I can't remember where." Eddie sat back, exhausted. "That's quite a gift, Taylor. Or I guess a curse depending on how you look at it."

Taylor's face darkened. "You could say that. It's something I have to live with. I have no choice." He looked up, his eyes panicked. "Promise me you won't tell anyone about this thing I have. You guys are my friends, so it was bound to come out sooner or later. Please don't tell anyone else."

Eddie shook his head gently even though his head was splitting. "We won't tell anyone, promise."

Taylor's face cleared, the look of relief evident.

Eddie leaned forward and touched Taylor's hand. "I for one am glad of your talent. You've saved us both now, and I'd hate to think what might have happened if you hadn't got your talent. It's truly incredible and you need to tell me more about it. But right now, I am so fucking tired." His heart thumped suddenly and he shot forward, his eyes wide. "Hell, I was supposed to go meet Gid—" he swallowed his words, not wanting to tell his friends he was going to a booty call with his boss. Leslie's plucked brows arched.

"Meet Gideon, were you going to say? Have you finally managed to get in that man's pants?"

Eddie flushed. "We had a moment earlier. I said I'd go back after close up and—" his voice tailed off at Leslie's grin.

"You were going to get laid, sweetheart!" Leslie crowed. "Oh how fortune has smiled upon our little Eddie."

"Shut up," Eddie growled. He touched his face gingerly. "I can't go over there looking like this. I'm a mess. Plus I honestly don't think I have it in me to have wild animal sex tonight."

"Oh, you definitely don't have it in you, *yet*," Leslie purred, his eyes sparkling. Taylor chuckled. Eddie cast a withering glance at his amused friends.

"Can it, you pervert. I'd better call him, tell him to take a rain check." He felt a pang of regret but he knew he wasn't in any mood to go across town and have Gideon see him all vulnerable and weak. He still felt ashamed that a pint-size man in heels had been the one to help rescue him.

"Did you say *rim* check?" Leslie said slyly and Taylor spluttered with laughter.

Eddie's mouth tugged. "Shut it you." He patted his pocket for his phone. "Shit, I forgot that asshole broke my phone. Did one of you pick it up at all?"

Taylor nodded and stood up to fetch his jacket. "Yeah, I got it. It's knackered though." He reached in the pocket and drew out Eddie's smashed and sorry looking mobile.

Eddie heaved a sigh. "Great. I'll have to try and call the restaurant directly and see if I can get hold of him or leave a message on the office phone. It's late so I doubt anyone will answer. I had his mobile number in there," he waved gloomily at the stricken phone. "And I'm not on shift tomorrow; it's my day off so I won't see him." Another thought struck him. "Shit, we're going to that dinner of yours tomorrow night, Leslie."

"Oh darling, it doesn't matter if you don't want to go and you'd rather see your man." Leslie's eyes shadowed though and there was no way Eddie was going to let him down after what he'd done for him tonight.

He shook his head firmly. "Uh-uh. I'm going with you and we are going to dance up a storm and show that miserable ex of yours exactly what he's missing." Leslie smiled, a sight that lit up the room. "Just give me a few hours' sleep and a shower and I'll be good to go."

He's not my man anyway. Not yet at least.

Eddie called the restaurant with Taylor's mobile—he'd been gracious enough to let Eddie use it in case he needed anything—and got the answering machine. It was almost midnight so he guessed Gideon might be upstairs in his flat already. He left a message saying something had happened and he needed to sort it out, and left Taylor's number, and that he'd see Gideon the day after tomorrow. Then a battered and slightly emotional Eddie dragged himself wearily off to bed.

He was rudely woken up by the shrill tones of the house phone lying on his bedside table. Blearily, Eddie peered at his bedside clock and winced. It was two a.m., for God's sake. Even if it were Gideon, this was not the time to be waking a man up.

"Hello?" he barked roughly into the phone.

A soft breathing was all that could be heard. Eddie squinted his eyes as if doing so would make him hear better. Daft he knew but it was a habit he had. "Hello, who is this?"

"It's me, cuz," was the faint reply.

"Luke? Do you know what fucking time it is?" Eddie's cousin Luke was seven years younger than him, a mix of geeky Tobey

Maguire meets Dylan O'Brien. He was also Eddie's best friend despite their age gap. He'd been the one person Eddie had really regretted leaving behind when he left Norfolk. Luke was a little highly strung and given to mood swings.

"Yeah, I know. I just—" Luke's whispered voice cut off and Eddie sat up, his senses on alert.

"Cuzbuster, is everything okay?" The old nickname bought back memories of the two of them drinking beer by the seashore, covered in sand as they got rather merry and then went for midnight dips in the freezing sea. The fact Eddie was supposed to be the mature one and he still let Luke drink alcohol at his tender age sometimes made him feel guilty. He also felt bad that he'd only been home twice in the past three months to visit his family and Luke in particular.

"Yeah, everything's fine, Red. I just wanted to hear your voice." Luke's voice was soft, and Eddie squinted more.

"It's pretty late, man. Have you been drinking? Is this a drunk-man call like those ones we used to pull when I was home?"

He and Luke had often made prank calls to people when they'd had a little too much to drink and had nothing better to do.

Luke's quiet laugh echoed in his year. "No, idiot. I just couldn't sleep and thought maybe you'd still be awake. I know you work some late shifts sometime."

"Okay, well this wasn't one of them. I was dreaming about giving some guy a really great blow job and you woke me up." Eddie grinned despite his initial ire at having his sleep disturbed. This was Luke after all. "How are things back home? Everything all right?"

There was silence then Luke replied. "Yeah, there's some stuff going on that maybe you can help me with but it can wait until you visit. You are planning on coming home soon, aren't you?"

"I thought I'd try get home for Halloween. I know you like that time of year and we can have some fun at the village bonfire. You know how we love messing about and scaring the kids to death."

"Oh, I thought it might be sooner than that. Never mind." Luke sounded tired and Eddie frowned.

"You don't sound yourself, Luke. What's going on, sunshine?"

Luke's tone sounded forced. "Nothing that can't wait until next month. I'll make sure we have the best pumpkins ready to carve for the competition. You know how Mum and Dad think we design the best ones for the fete. We can't let them down." There was a rustling, like newspaper, or the pages of a book. "Anyway I'll go and let you get back to sleep. I'll call you soon, unless you call me first."

"Okay, yeah, I'll give you a ring soon. Oh and give a kiss to Rachel for me. Tell her I'll see her soon too." Rachel was Luke's girlfriend. They'd been going out for four months now and while Eddie hadn't got to know her that well before he'd left, he'd liked the seventeen-year-old brunette.

"Erm, sure, I'll do that. Listen, I'd better go. Speak soon, Red." The phone went dead and Eddie laid it back on the bed side table. He felt a little unsettled as if something was wrong but he couldn't put his finger on it. As he snuggled down under his duvet to try and get back to sleep, he decided to try get back home a little sooner than planned. It sounded like Luke needed him.

Chapter 9

Gideon stormed across the restaurant floor wishing he could hit something to rid himself of the temper bubbling inside him. He felt like a fool, a stupid, "I should have known better" fool. He'd rushed around like a crazy man last night in preparation for Eddie's visit. He'd closed up the restaurant in record time; had a shower, shaved and put on his best pair of jeans—the ones with the buttons, as there was something about a man unbuttoning them slowly that did things to him. His tee shirt had been just right, hugging his body and the contours of the muscles he had, and he was ready and raring to go. And then the little wanker hadn't even bothered to show up. Gideon had sat up drinking wine until two a.m., even though he'd known Eddie was a no show. He hadn't even called and Gideon hadn't got his number. He'd gone to bed horny, jerked off and fallen into an uneasy sleep, populated by images of fire, burning bodies and angels bearing Eddie's face cackling as they flew around in the skies taunting him.

Eddie wasn't on the duty roster today and there'd still been no sign of him, telephonically or otherwise. Gideon should have known better. He should have stuck to his original instinct of not mixing business and pleasure. Well, he wouldn't be making that mistake again. He chomped down fiercely on his piece of gum wishing it was Eddie he was chewing out. He plucked at the rubber band on his wrist, drawing it away then letting it go to leave a stinging mark on his skin. It was one way to manage the panic attacks that sometimes threatened. He hadn't had to use one for a while but lately…things were different.

Carmen laid a hand on his arm as he stalked past her. "Hey, Gideon, you all right?" her black eyes were concerned. "You look pissed off and as if you haven't slept again."

"I'm fine," Gideon snapped. "Just have a lot on my mind. I'm going to the kitchen to speak to Jerome. If you see Sarah can you tell her that I've arranged for the Goodwins to go on table four? They're the one with that hyperactive kid and that's the best place to put them so he doesn't disrupt the other diners."

"Sure, honey. I'll tell her." Gideon felt Carmen's eyes on him as he entered the kitchen. The staff waved and smiled at him and not wanting to be churlish, he managed a grin and a few words. Jerome was busy at the stove with scallops and what looked like strips of juicy, thick pork belly. He turned as Gideon tapped him on the shoulder and his face split into a huge toothy grin.

"Gideon! Good to see you here, my friend. What's up?" He turned back to the sizzling dish on the stove. Gideon's chest tightened at the easy demeanour of the man cooking, taking it so for granted that he could smell the aromas in the kitchen, the energising scents of herbs, spices and meats, taste them in the back of the throat, taste buds watering and ready to consume the delights that were offered.

Gideon's hand clenched as he replied. "I was asked by one of the patrons if you'd like to go out to the front—table eleven? He said he loved your spinach roulade so much he'd like to pay his compliments." Gideon's stomach plummeted. There'd been a time when *he'd* been the one going out to greet satisfied patrons but he'd never begrudge Jerome his moment of glory.

Jerome beamed as he wafted the spatula he clutched in a big hand around in front of Gideon's face. A blob of something flew off and hit Gideon's cheek and he raised a finger and wiped it off, then instinctively put it in his mouth the clean off. It was wet, warm—and that was it. He had no idea what he'd just eaten. He picked up a dishcloth and wiped whatever it had been off his cheek. He dropped the cloth down next to him on the surface idly as his mind raced.

Jerome nodded. "Well, that's a lovely surprise. Sure, let me finish up here and then I'll pop over to table eleven." He turned to his still cooking dish and poked it around a bit. Gideon watched him for a minute, seeing the tantalising brown of the scallops as they seared, appreciating the pale gold hue of the butter as they cooked.

Jerome turned with a faint scowl on his face and then sniffed loudly. "What the hell is that smell?" Suddenly the kitchen was rent by the sound of the smoke alarm, a shrill, irritating beep. People glanced around wildly, trying to detect the problem. Jerome's eyes darted to Gideon's side and they widened. "Shit, Gideon, the dishtowel is burning."

Gideon's face turned towards the source of Jerome's concern and saw the dishtowel smouldering, starting to smoke and flame. Bile and panic rising in his throat, he reached out quickly and plucked it from where it lay, still on the stove top plate that no doubt had still been hot. He dropped it hastily into the kitchen sink, which was still full of sudsy water. The fiery dishtowel fizzled out.

Gideon's body flushed with heat that firstly he had been so careless and that secondly, he hadn't smelt the dishcloth burning. He gazed down at the wet dishcloth with eyes that didn't really see and Jerome laid a meaty hand on his. Gideon looked up to see a pair of brown eyes regarding him compassionately. He thought they might be seeing directly into his withered soul. One of the kitchen staff was flapping another large dishtowel at the offending and still trilling smoke alarm in an effort to stop it. Finally the kitchen was silent.

Jerome gazed at Gideon, his eyes soft. "Nothing we can't fix, boss. Dishtowels are a dime a dozen in this kitchen. And thank God for smoke detectors. It's not the first time we've had that happen."

Gideon nodded. He felt sick. What if he'd done that at home? He could have caused a fire, burnt the restaurant down, hurt people. Bile rose in his throat and he nodded jerkily. Then he turned and got out of the kitchen as fast as he could. He walked blindly to his office and sat behind his desk, staring blankly around his office. And *that* in a nutshell was the reason why he didn't work in a kitchen anymore. He was fucking useless. Tears pricked at the back of his eyes and he blinked them away fiercely. A noise at the door made him look up.

Carmen smiled at him. "Sarah says thanks for the heads up. She says the Goodwins are all settled and little Jeremiah is under control with the colouring books and Lego kit you left for him. That was a sweet gesture."

"Yes, well it distracts him and keeps him busy. He's a nice kid, just a little manic." Gideon chewed rapidly as he picked up a sheaf of papers not wanting to see the expression of what he thought was pity in Carmen's eyes. No doubt by now she'd have heard of his stupid fuck-up in the kitchen. "I've got some paperwork to sort out so I'll be out on the floor in a minute."

"Okie-dokie, honey. Oh by the way, remember I'm leaving a little earlier today from my shift. You okayed it last week. I said to Eddie I'd pick up his tux on my home and drop it off at his place. He's only a few blocks away from me and it saves him coming in today on his day off. I tried to call Eddie today to remind him but I can't get through. It goes straight to voice mail." She grinned. "And I'm not in tomorrow, remember. Day off."

Gideon remembered then that Eddie was accompanying his "friend" to some fancy dinner. "Oh yes," he muttered. "Far be it for Eddie to make it back this way for any reason. Or call anyone." He winced even as he said the words.

I sound like a bloody teenager being stood up on prom night.

Carmen wandered into the office, looking all innocent but Gideon knew her too well. She was a piranha, with teeth that were able to dig under his skin and make him bleed with her concern.

"Sounding a little peeved there, G? Is everything all right in paradise?" Her brows rose in query.

"Everything's fine. I'm here, you're here, what could possibly be wrong?" Bitterness leaked out of his mouth like toxic waste. "Now be off with you and leave me alone. I've got work to do." He pulled the pile of paperwork toward him with intent and ignored Carmen.

She sighed heavily. "Fine. I shall leave you to get on with whatever you're not doing. And Gideon?"

He looked up at her in exasperation. "What?"

"Cut yourself some slack. Please." She disappeared. Gideon let out a breath and leaned back in his chair.

Concentrate, Gideon. Forget Eddie, getting laid and anything else. Just focus on work. It's all you need to do right now.

*****

The following morning Gideon knew Eddie was on a double shift. He deliberately stayed away from the kitchen, not wanting to hear any discussions or scuttlebutt about his burning dishcloth affair. He still flushed every time he thought about it. It was a particularly busy day, and the restaurant was a chaotic amount of people in and out the doors. It was close to six that evening when he finally had a break and went out to the back alley for some fresh air. He missed the act of smoking, of coming out here with the other smokers and shooting the breeze. He'd tried to join them and simply enjoy their company but the sight of them all so obviously enjoying their smoke break pissed him off a little. So now he and his packet of gum stood outside. He was about to throw his current piece away in the dumpster when he heard a low cough. He turned to see Eddie standing there, smiling at him. Immediately Gideon scowled and his fingers nervously moved to his rubber band. He fingered it, noticing Eddie's face, the cut on his cheek, and the bruising. He felt a twinge of concern, wondering what had happened but he was in too bad a mood to simply ask about it like a caring person would. Instead he went on the attack.

"Had a really good time last night then? Have a little bit of trouble in the bathroom—didn't you want to give it up?" he said scathingly.

Eddie's eyes widened. "What? No, nothing like that." He flushed pinkly. "What the hell do you mean by that anyway?" His smile had disappeared.

Gideon shrugged. "Looks like you had to fight them off, or maybe made the wrong move." He knew he was being a total prick but his ire was seething and wanted out. "The sight of you in a tux too good to resist then? Like those damn leathers you had on the other night. Nothing says 'I'm available' like those ones did." He flicked his gum into the bin then snapped the band against his wrist, uttering a slight hiss of pain at the sting.

Eddie stepped toward him, his body taut. "What the fuck is wrong with you? Why are you being such an arsehole?" His voice was tight.

"It's in my nature, Eddie. I don't like being stood up. It brings out the nasty in me." He saw Eddie about to speak and shook his head. "I'm not interested in why you didn't come back. I guess you found something better to do. And so have I. It was probably for the best anyway. It'd never have worked. So maybe I should thank you for not coming around for a fucking."

Eddie swallowed, his green eyes filled with hurt and confusion. "Gideon, I—"

Gideon swept past him and went back into the restaurant. He'd said his bit although he felt sick. He'd never set out before to hurt someone deliberately like he'd just done to Eddie.

Christ, what the hell is wrong with me? Have I just completely lost it?

He was still wondering that when he finally went to bed that night with a stinging wrist, his gut churning, his head aching, and with a sense of self-hatred he'd never felt before.

Chapter 10

The following morning didn't start all that well for Gideon. He'd had a really bad night and ended up puking into the toilet after a particularly bad dream.

"You fucking selfish prick. What the hell is wrong with you?"

Gideon glanced up in amazement at a spitting mad Carmen, who stood with hands on hips in front of him halfway down the steps as he cleaned the beer lines in the quiet, dimly lit basement of Galileo's.

He frowned. "Hell, it's a good thing we're friends, Carmen, or I might have to fire your arse for spouting off at me like that. What the hell is your problem?" He rubbed his wrist, noting absently that he hadn't put the band on after his shower.

Carmen glowered. "What bug is up your arse that you had to say those things to Eddie yesterday? He didn't deserve it. Did he actually get to tell you what happened the night he missed your booty call, Gideon? Did you at least let him explain what went down?"

Gideon stood up, wincing as his back complained from being hunched down. "I know enough. He—"

"You know nothing!" Gideon was amazed to see Carmen's eyes glittering with tears. "Someone attacked him, Gideon. Tried to force him on his knees to give them a blow job then smacked him around. If it hadn't been for his friends seeing what was going on, he might have been badly hurt. The man had a knife at Eddie's face, for God's sake."

Gideon's body went cold. His heart threatened to plummet to his stomach and join the acid coiling around his innards. "What?"

"Oh, very good comeback, arsehole." Carmen clattered down to the bottom of the steps and stood in front of him. "He was all shook up and his phone was smashed when he was attacked. So he didn't have your mobile number. He left a message on the phone in the office. But I bet you didn't check, did you?"

Gideon hadn't checked the messages in fact. It was one of those jobs he was terrible at doing. He could only stand there and listen to both the self-recriminations flooding his brain and Carmen spouting off. His fingers tingled and he tried taking deep breaths to calm himself down.

I can do this. I don't need a fucking rubber band.

Carmen's face was a picture of disappointment. At Gideon.

"He tried to tell us he'd fallen and hit a wall, but you know me, I have ways of ferreting out the truth. He's absolutely bloody miserable about what you said to him."

Gideon stood, hearing Carmen but not listening to her words. The shame he felt at mouthing off and causing Eddie's distress on top of what he'd already suffered mortified him. He could only watch Carmen's mouth move while he figured out how to make this better.

Finally Carmen ran out of steam. She stood, bosom heaving, as she glared at him again.

Gideon sank down onto the cold stone bench in the cellar and buried his face in his hands. Then he looked up at his friend. "I'll apologise to him," he said huskily. "Is he still here?"

She nodded. "Yes. He's knocking off at five. You'd better find him and make this right, G. He's a bit of a mess. The police had to re-interview him because the man who attacked him said he paid for the blow job, and then Eddie tried to rob *him*. I don't think it will stick but being painted as a rent boy isn't helping."

Gideon closed his eyes. "I promise I'll make this right," he agreed quietly. "No matter what. Can you please do me a favour and get him to my office somehow? I have the feeling if I ask him he'll just refuse. I don't want to do anything in front of the others either."

Carmen narrowed her eyes. "I'll think of something." She turned and walked up the stairs, turning back to look at him gently. "You need help, Gideon. This isn't you, this bad-tempered bastard. You need to talk to someone about the accident and the nightmares. Before you have a breakdown, honey. Please say you will at least consider it."

Gideon huffed a breath. "I don't need—"

"Yes, you do," Carmen said, her face wreathed in sympathy. "It needs to be addressed." She went up the stairs and didn't look back. Gideon finished what he was doing in silence, his body numb as he went through the motions. His hands were freezing, his mind dull. Finally he ascended the stairs, switched off the light and made his way through the restaurant to his office. He was an autopilot, stopping to talk to one or two of the regulars, chatting to Sarah and complimenting some of the waitstaff scurrying about. Eventually he walked into his office to see Eddie bent over the printer once more.

He turned as Gideon came in. Gideon closed the door and locked it. His heart lurched at the sight of the bruise on Eddie's face, and the thin red line of the cut on his cheek. Eddie's normally beautiful and pale skin was marked with brutality and Gideon felt a seething of hatred for the man who had done it.

Eddie regarded him expressionlessly. "Carmen said you were busy and the printer was acting up. I seem to be the fix it man for some reason. But it looks fine to me." His eyebrows rose. "Why is the door locked?"

"Because I owe you an apology and I wanted to do this privately without an interruption." Gideon perched his arse on the corner of his desk as he looked at Eddie with resolve. He wanted to lean over and kiss the damage on Eddie's face but wasn't sure he had that right. He'd probably get smacked but he thought it would be worth it. Definitely worth it, he mused.

Eddie's lips curled. "I think it's a bit late for that. You had your say. Now if you don't mind, I need to get back to work." He moved past Gideon and Gideon caught his upper arm.

Eddie yanked it away, his face angry. "Let me alone," he warned. "You know what they say about red heads and tempers? Well they were talking about me when my gander is up. Don't fucking mess with me."

Gideon might have been feeling like the world's shittiest arsehole but he still thought Eddie was absolutely adorable. His pale, marked face was flushed with colour, freckles standing out across the bridge of his nose. His green eyes were like chips of green bottle glass, and his biceps had felt like steel when Gideon had grabbed him. He still wanted to kiss the crap out of this man. He also knew he had to say his piece quickly.

"I need to tell you how sorry I am," Gideon murmured. "I was a complete dipshit. You didn't deserve what I said and I didn't mean it. I have no idea how to make you believe me. If you want me on my knees apologising, I'll do it. Whatever you need me to do to make this better, just ask."

"According to you I'm the one on my knees." Eddie's voice was acidic. "And the

police thought so too. It took everything we had to convince them I wasn't a prostitute. Oh, wait, I forget. You didn't know about my brush with a molester did you, the night I was supposed to meet you?" His voice shook.

Gideon swallowed. "I heard about it from Carmen. In no uncertain terms, let me tell you." Thoughts of kissing Eddie fled from his head at the disgusted expression on Eddie's face.

"Yes, well. Carmen's a good friend." Eddie's tone was uncompromising, leaving Gideon in no doubt that *he* wasn't. "I see what you think of me now though, and in all honesty, we should simply leave it there. Thanks for the apology."

He turned, unlocked the door and marched out of the office.

*****

Two days later Gideon could bear it no longer. He was a nervous wreck. He was hyper sensitive to Eddie's presence—watching him stride across the floor of the restaurant from stock room to kitchen, seeing him go into the kitchen staff room to change before catching his train home and catching sight of his studious frame hard at work every time Gideon went into the kitchen. Eddie did his best to ignore him too, but Gideon knew he was watching him. He'd felt Eddie's eyes on his back and when he turned around, they'd be elsewhere.

Eddie must have the quickest damn reflexes, Gideon mused darkly. He was like some bloody sneaky ginger-haired tomcat that spat and clawed and then simply affected an air of disdain as if a person wasn't there. Gideon snorted. Typical cat. He was a dog man himself.

It was driving him completely crazy and there was no way he wanted this friction between them. So Gideon did what any red-blooded man needing to fix things in a non-relationship would do. He waylaid Eddie in the staff room one night late after work, when all of the rest of the kitchen employees were gone.

Eddie's habit was generally to be the last one to leave. He'd disappear to get out of his smelly kitchen clobber into comfortable jeans and sweatshirt and then wrap his old suede jacket round his lithe body before he hot-footed it for his train. It was easy enough for Gideon to wait and then make sure no one else was in there before sneaking in behind him and locking the door.

I don't give a damn what anyone thinks. This is my bloody restaurant and they can deal with me if they don't like it.

At the click of the door closing, Eddie turned in surprise and his face darkened when he saw Gideon standing there, trying to look as contrite as possible. He even fixed a smile on his face in the hope Eddie might feel more susceptible to his charms.

"Gideon? What are you doing here?" His voice was husky and Gideon heard a slight wariness.

"It's my restaurant. I can be here if I want to."

Oh, so damn smooth, you stupid tosser.

Gideon wanted to kick himself for that airy reply. "We have some unfinished business, Eddie." No sooner were *those* words out than Gideon wanted to claw them back.

Way to phrase that one, Kent. It sounds like you expect him to fall to his knees and give you that blow job you always wanted.

Eddie's eyes narrowed, a flush rising on the pale cheeks and he took a step forward, fists clenched. "Honestly? *Unfinished business?*"

Gideon winced. "That didn't quite come out the way I wanted it to. I meant we need to talk. A bit more. If that's all right with you." He was gabbling now and perhaps he should shut his mouth.

Eddie regarded him with suspicion. "I thought we'd said what we had to already."

"No, you said what *you* had to say then walked away. You didn't give me a chance to explain more."

He moved closer to Eddie. Eddie watched him carefully, his lips trembling. Gideon sensed he was a little on edge, uncertain of where this was going. So he did something that completely surprised them both. He took Eddie's face gently between his hands and kissed him. Tentatively, slowly, brushing his lips against Eddie's cool ones, trying to impart the apology and guilt he felt in that one single caress of lips on lips. He braced himself for a punch, for Eddie to shift away. Instead Eddie sighed, warm breath on Gideon's face and Gideon had to physically hold himself back from pulling Eddie into him, taking his mouth violently and thrusting his own hardness against what he knew would be reciprocated. Gideon laid his forehead against Eddie's as his thumbs traced Eddie's jaw.

"I'm so sorry for what happened to you," he whispered raggedly. "I'm glad you had friends to come to your rescue. I couldn't bear the thought of you being hurt." He pulled back then placed a gentle kiss next to the cut on Eddie's cheek.

Eddie was still, his eyes staring into Gideon's with an intensity that made his groin ache and his heart beat faster.

Gideon moved away a little. "I'm sorry I was such a bastard." He brushed a stray strand of hair from Eddie's eyes, relieved that Eddie hadn't pushed him away. He had a feeling he would have, had the situation been reversed.

"What is this, G?" Eddie asked quietly. "This thing we have…" His hands slowly moved to Gideon's shirt and he smoothed the fabric idly over his chest, causing turmoil in Gideon's body. He loved the diminutive of his name reduced to one single letter by this man who played havoc with his emotions.

"I have no idea," Gideon confessed. "I've never felt this way for someone before. Thought about anyone like I do you."

Eddie smiled and Gideon's world instantly got to be a better place. "Ditto."

He traced Gideon's lips with his finger tips and then pressed his mouth to his, harder and more possessive than the original kiss had been. Eddie licked along Gideon's lower lip and pushed into his mouth, eager, greedy.

Gideon was lost. He'd dreamed of this for so long, this crush he had on this flame-haired, sexy man. Now that he had him in his arms, he never wanted to let go. It was crazy, groin-tinglingly over the top, "are you fucking mad" bat-shit confusing, but it was all Gideon needed and wanted right now. He gripped Eddie's round, tight arse cheeks, pulling him against his front and Eddie whimpered in his mouth as he ground himself against Gideon, his hardness pressing into his own.

That whimper sent shades of vibrant colour to Gideon's closed eyes, a surge of heat to his already throbbing dick, and his body shivered with pure animal need at the hard-muscled strength of the man in his arms. The man who was currently trying to reach Gideon's tonsils with his searching tongue and whose warm fingers trailed licks of fire down Gideon's spine and skin. Somewhere along the line, Gideon's shirt had come unbuttoned, his trousers had been unzipped and now a hand stroked his hardened prick through the thin fabric of his cotton boxers.

Gideon could no longer think straight. The world suddenly seemed a smaller place, shrunk to a universe of two people, skin to skin—somehow Eddie's shirt was also rucked up under his armpits—and as Gideon fought desperately to absorb Eddie into his body using his own backside as an instrument to draw him in, the fact he couldn't smell or taste this man was eclipsed by the fact that he could *feel* him in every cell in his body.

Under Gideon's fingertips, beneath his loose trousers, the skin of Eddie's arse was dimpled with goose bumps. His hair was soft against Gideon's face, the stubble that coated Eddie's chin and upper lip grazed Gideon's cheek and jaw. The noises Eddie was making as he kissed the crap out of Gideon were a turn-on beyond belief. Gideon's remaining senses ran riot, the sensory overload making him dizzy with need.

He needed to breathe, so he pulled his lips away from where they were being devoured, then pulled back to see Eddie's swollen pink mouth and glittering green eyes regarding him with a lustful fervour that he made no effort to mask. Gideon felt a sense of egotistical pride in causing that type of reaction in the man panting before him.

"Eddie, let's just slow this down," he gasped, needing to get some sense into his head even though his body was screaming for more. "This is work and we can't really do this here. Not everything I want to do to you anyway."

Eddie drew a shuddering breath. "Is this another rain check? Because I have to tell you, that whole idea sucks." His lips curled in a wolfish grin. "As do I."

He knelt down before Gideon, red hair tousled, cheeks pink and without any hesitation, he pushed Gideon's trousers and underwear down to his knees then engulfed Gideon's dick in a hot, wet mouth. All Gideon's sanity departed in a rush of blood to the very organ currently being assaulted with loving and desperate care.

"Oh-my-fucking-God," he managed to get out before losing the power of speech completely and splaying his hands in Eddie's hair, pushing his mouth deeper onto his dick in the hope that maybe that way they may both be better assimilated into each other. Because, really, he wanted to wear Eddie like a second skin. There was no way he was stopping now. Half of the patrons of Galileo's could have walked in to find Eddie blowing him and he would simply have ignored them all.

He watched Eddie's mouth around his prick, that decadent, fat-lipped mouth bobbing up and down on him like a ship at sea. Eddie raised his eyes to look at him, eyes that were half hidden behind swathes of flame-coloured hair to match the fire in his eyes, and Gideon felt the incredible pressure in his balls, the flood of fluid into his prick, and he cried out loudly as he filled Eddie's tempting mouth with the warm wash of his seed. His body shuddered and jerked like a man with a fever, and he gripped Eddie's head tighter. He stood, trembling, his legs boneless limbs, as Eddie stood up, a wide grin on his face and his own cock pushing out of his black-and-white-checked trousers like a Big Top circus tent-pole.

"My turn," he whispered, voice sultry, and Gideon stared as his fingers were raised to Eddie's mouth. Eddie took his time sucking each one of them in turn then licking Gideon's palm until it was wet. Gideon's breath deepened as his hand was pushed southwards and Eddie's intent was perfectly clear.

Gideon growled softly as he pulled Eddie's pants down onto lean, pale-skinned hips and wrapped his hand around Eddie's cock. "How do you like it—slow, hard, fast? Tell me, Eddie." He began jerking him off to soft moans from Eddie's punished pink lips.

"Just like that," Eddie hissed as he once again found Gideon's mouth and proceeded to ravage it again. Time seemed to cease in the office, and Gideon's only focus was the hot flesh in his hand, the slickness of fluid coating his fingers and palm, the groans and pants from the man thrusting his tongue in his mouth and his own breathlessness as Eddie tensed against him and wet, sticky come cascaded over his hand and wrist. Eddie collapsed against him, his mouth tickling Gideon's neck.

"Oh God," he breathed into Gideon's ear. "That was pretty fucking awesome, I have to tell you. Your hands are magic."

They stared at each other and Gideon ran a hand through Eddie's sweating hair. "I'm glad you're okay," he murmured. "The thought of that bastard touching you, forcing you to do things to him—I want to bloody kill him myself. Are you sure it's safe now for you out there now?"

Eddie reached up and caressed his cheek gently. "He's in custody. I'm sure he's not daft enough to come after me again." He pressed soft lips to Gideon's and he closed his eyes, revelling in the feeling.

"I just wish I could taste you," he whispered to Eddie. "Smell you. You have no idea how much I miss it."

Eddie sighed gently. "You can feel and hear me, G. Right here, right now. Feel my fingers in your hair, my mouth on yours, feel my body against you. Hear my breath and my voice. Concentrate on those senses instead." He pressed himself closer. Gideon's breath hitched at the sensation of warm, hard man. "You can see me. Watch my face when you make me feel so good."

Gideon groaned and found Eddie's mouth again, bruising his lips in his intensity to absorb the man. A sudden hard knock at the locked door bought them to their senses and they moved apart quickly.

"Eddie, are you in there? Why's the door locked? You're going to miss your train if you don't hurry up."

"Christ, is she still here?" Gideon said in a panic. "Don't any of my staff go home on time?"

Sarah's voice sounded amused and Gideon couldn't help wondering just how much she knew of his infatuation for Eddie. He knew she and Carmen were good work friends and he was sure that his crush wouldn't have gone unspoken about when the two women got together.

"Just a minute," he called out as he hastily tucked himself away and watched Eddie do the same. He motioned around the room with his hand. "Does it smell of sex in here?" he hissed. Eddie sniffed then grimaced. "Yeah, pretty much reeks of it. Have you any air freshener?"

"No, I don't have bloody air freshener, what does this look like, a damn hotel?" Gideon gazed about him, wild eyed.

Eddie sighed. "*And* he's back. Mr. Fucking Grumpy." His eyes darted around the room. "Wait. Someone keeps deodorant in here, I think." He opened a desk drawer and picked up a can of Lynx Dry Twist spray. He sprayed it liberally around the room.

Gideon hissed at Eddie. "Open the door and try and act like we haven't just—well, done what we just did."

"You mean the blow job and jerk-off?" Eddie said drily as he unlocked the door. "I have no problem not sharing that."

Sarah marched in and the wicked smile she gave made his heart beat faster with panic.

"Having a little bit of a sweat problem in here, lads?" Her grin was knowing. "You need to watch that." She fanned herself. "Boy, it's hot in here."

Gideon regarded her warily. "Eddie and I were just…talking." He knew it was a lame excuse and from Eddie's soft snigger, he did too.

Sarah chuckled. "Of course you were." Her eyes glinted mischievously. "I just thought I should remind Eddie about his train. Plus I still have your credit card in my bag from lunchtime when I paid the suppliers. I needed to give it back before you left and I thought I might find you both in here." She handed over Gideon's credit card with a smirk.

He scowled as he put it in his trouser pocket.

Eddie moved toward the door and Gideon tried to catch his eye. Eddie nodded at him but there was a knowing glint in his eye. "See you later, boss. I've got a train to catch." He disappeared out the door. Gideon was left with Sarah who was all but sniggering.

"So," she drawled. "You and Eddie, huh? Who would have guessed?" Her face clearly showed that she definitely would have guessed.

Gideon scowled again. He seemed to be doing that a lot lately and he really needed to stop it before he got lines on his face. "What's between Eddie and me is none of your business, nosey parker," he said loftily.

Sarah pursed her lips. "Oh, indeed, boss man." She turned with a giggle and disappeared out the door. Gideon heaved a sigh of relief.

Well that all hadn't gone too badly. He was back on an even keel with Eddie and had released some of the sexual tension he'd had. Gideon still wasn't sure that this thing with Eddie was a good idea but he didn't think it could be avoided. The chemistry between them was too intense. Gideon felt a prickle of unease down his spine. The feelings he harboured for his red-haired chef seemed to be more than sexual attraction. When he'd been kissing Eddie, he'd felt very at home in the man's mouth and holding him in his arms. It had almost felt like home.

Chapter 11

Eddie was flying high in the kitchen the next day. He buzzed around it like a darting dragonfly, feeling the goofy smile on his face as he worked. He'd only broken two glasses and Jerome had given him the evil eye for a while, but then he'd relented on seeing Eddie in a better mood. Instead he'd merely warned him airily that if he broke anything else today he'd shove his fist down Eddie's throat. Eddie had simply nodded and agreed that was fine.

The day passed swiftly, Eddie's shift coming to an end all too soon at six o'clock. He'd hoped to manage to see Gideon again, to find out whether they could get together that night, but so far Jerome had kept him so busy, there'd been no time. Gideon had come into the kitchen once or twice, glancing at Eddie, almost as if reassuring himself that Eddie was still there. Eddie liked that feeling; the one that said someone cared about him enough to be a little possessive. Each time he saw Gideon's lithe frame and broad shoulders in view, his nether regions tingled and his skin prickled with longing.

Eddie had it bad.

He felt his new mobile vibrate in his pocket. It was a message from his cousin Luke.

Hi Red. Hw r thngs with u?

Eddie texted back. He had a real dislike of text speak, probably because he'd had one very strict and anal retentive English teacher in college who had constantly lectured on the correct use of language. She had despised the whole shortened text and email speech, saying it made students lazy and unable to spell. Eddie tended to agree with her but he'd never told her that. She would have hauled him to the front of the class with a smirk and embarrassed the shit out of him.

Good thanks. What are you up to?

There was a delay then *Ok. U stll cmg back 31st?*

Eddie remembered he'd told Luke he'd be home for Halloween.

Think so. Going to try.

Gd. Need to tlk. Spk then.

Okay. See you soon. Tell Rachel hi.

Eddie popped his phone back in his pocket. He frowned. Luke was certainly being very attentive. Twice in one week he'd contacted

Eddie when normally the little git had to be forced to keep in touch. Something was up and when he got home he'd find out what.

He finished cleaning up and said goodbye to his colleagues then made his way to the change room. He'd just changed into jeans and a comfy tee shirt and was busy stuffing his dirty whites into his rucksack when he heard a cough behind him. He turned to see Carmen grinning at him.

"Did you two kiss and make up then?" she asked.

Eddie's face warmed. "Yes, I guess we did."

Carmen flapped a hand. "About damn time, you two stubborn arseholes." She came closer. "So everything is okay now between you two? No more miserable Eddie and grumpy Gideon?"

Eddie sniggered. "No, no more Mr. GG." He frowned and rummaged around in his pocket. He drew out his phone and looked at Carmen. "Do me a favour and give me Gideon's mobile number. I just got this new phone yesterday and I need to put all the numbers back in."

Carmen reached over and plucked the phone from Eddie's hand. "Let me pop it in for you now." She deftly pressed the buttons as Eddie watched then handed it back to him with a satisfied smirk. "There you go. It's filed under 'Booty Call.'"

Eddie chuckled. "Really, that's the best you could do?" He put his phone back in his pocket and hefted his bag onto his shoulder. "I'll give him a call later then."

Carmen's face softened. "I'm glad about you and the boss. He needs someone right now. He won't talk about that night of the fire to anyone and he bottles it all up inside. The fact he had to give up cooking—that killed him. It festers inside him and he needs to move on. Maybe you can make him see that."

"I'm not sure we're there yet," Eddie said quietly. "I mean, I like the guy but I doubt he's ready to share his man angst with me yet. Hell, I don't even know what's going on. This could just be all about sex. But I'll let him know if he needs to talk, I'll be there."

He moved toward the door. He wanted to pop by and see if Gideon was in his office before he left and whether he had plans for the night. It was Friday after all. "I'll see you Monday then, as I'm on late tomorrow and you don't work Saturdays. Enjoy the weekend." He left Carmen behind and sauntered down to Gideon's office. The man wasn't in there or in the restaurant. Eddie sighed.

Okay, well I'll give him a call later. I don't want to be too needy or I might scare him off.

His ride on the tube was coupled with both anxiety and a little bit of fear. Eddie found himself studying the people around him, assessing who might be a threat and who might be giving him the eye. He hated that he felt this insecure. When he got to his stop and stepped onto the platform, he glanced behind him to make sure no one was following him. The walk home was fraught with dangerous possibilities; every alleyway, every homeless bum knocking into him, every person that was big and beefy looked like a threat. He was very glad when he reached the front gate to his home and made his way inside. He closed the door behind him with a sigh of relief and plopped his backpack onto the floor in the entrance.

When he walked into the kitchen he found Leslie with a spatula in hand, earbuds in and dancing around the kitchen as he cooked pasta. His flatmate looked relaxed in a pair of low-hanging blue sweatpants and an oversized tee shirt with the words, "Sperm whales blow and so do I" written all over the back. Eddie choked back a laugh and tapped Leslie on the shoulder. Leslie shrieked and the spatula went flying across the kitchen to land on the floor.

"Oh my God, you scared the fuck out of me," Leslie hissed as he pulled his buds out of his ears. Eddie heard the tinny sounds of Lady Gaga blaring out of them.

Eddie peered into the boiling pots on the stove. Billows of fragrant steam blew into his face and he smelt the tantalising aroma of garlic and basil. He felt a pang at the fact that he took it for granted he could smell it. He knew that if he too were to lose his sense of smell and taste, part of who he was as a chef would be irretrievably lost.

"Smells great," he remarked. "Are you expecting company? There seems to be lot of it."

Leslie bent down to retrieve his spatula and shook his head. His wavy black hair bobbed on his head, coifed as it was into thick, elegant curls. "No, it's just you, me and Taylor. He should be home soon. That damn music shop he works at is making him work double shifts this week because one of the guys is sick. As if they don't get their pound of flesh from him anyway." He busied himself lifting pan lids and stirring what looked to Eddie like a ragout of creamy chicken and mushrooms.

Eddie stared at Leslie in disbelief. "It's Friday night. Shouldn't you be getting ready to go out partying instead of being Momma Bear Cook?"

Leslie huffed as he turned to stare Eddie down, his blue eyes ringed with mascara. "Even we party animals like a night off now and then, you know. And I thought after all the action this week with you being attacked and nearly violated, we should have a home-cooked meal, drink some beer and chill out together. I didn't think you had plans." The unspoken *You never have plans anyway* wasn't lost on Eddie. Leslie looked at Eddie anxiously. "Oh God, you *did* have plans, didn't you? I'm going to have to eat this whole damn pot of chicken stroganoff by myself. Then I'll put on twenty pounds, get fat and no one will look at me twice. I'll end my years as a fat, frumpy old maid with no man to share it with because he can't get near my dick for the fat rolls." Leslie's tirade of words only stopped because Eddie placed a firm finger on his glossy lips to shut him up.

"It's fine. I had no plans yet so eating in sounds good to me. I just need a shower first." Thoughts of what he might do in the shower thinking of Gideon made him smile.

Leslie's gazed at him curiously. "You seem in a really good mood these days, Eddie…" His voice trailed off and he looked at Eddie with wide eyes. "Oh my God, you totally had sex with your boss, didn't you? I think I can smell the pheromones seeping out of your body." He tapped the side of his nose with the spatula, leaving a small glob of cream on it. "You know this proboscis of mine is a fine tuning fork, boyfriend. And this nose is telling me you got laid. Was it that gorgeous boss of yours?"

Leslie's nose was indeed a marvel of the modern world. There wasn't a man alive who could wear a cheap eau de cologne around him and hope to pass it off as anything other than what it was.

Eddie reached over and scooped the glob from Leslie's nose with the tip of his finger. He wiped it on the dishtowel. "I gave him a blow job and he jacked me off in his office yesterday. So I guess that constitutes sex." He smiled. "And honestly, proboscis?"

Leslie squealed and hugged Eddie, warm arms wrapping themselves around his waist as he plastered kisses on Eddie's cheek.

"Awesome. I'm so glad. You two seem to have been dithering about it for ages." He unpeeled himself from Eddie and turned his attention back to the simmering contents of the pot. "You'll have to tell me and Taylor all about it when we eat. I'm dying for all the details." He waved his spatula. "Now shoo. Off you go and get yourself all cleaned up before supper."

Eddie rolled his eyes but went to do as he was told.

An hour later he was lying on his bed, still wet and clad in nothing but a towel when his phone rang. He peered at the screen. *Booty Call.*

Eddie felt the grin split his face as he answered. "Hi, Gideon."

"You knew it was me? You have me programmed in your phone?" Gideon sounded surprised but pleased. Eddie snorted. He wasn't about to tell him about his call sign.

"Of course I have your number." He noticed the flirty tone of his voice and cringed.

Way to be cool, Eddie. Tip the man off just how much you want him.

"I'm sorry I didn't get to see you before you left. Carmen said you came looking for me." A deep sigh echoed down the phone. "Some kid locked himself in the bathroom in a strop and I had to coax him out using only my incredible charm and the promise of a free knickerbocker glory when he finally deigned to come out."

Eddie chuckled. "A knickerbocker glory would entice anyone out of seclusion. It's one of my favourite puddings."

"That's good to know when I want to tempt you." Gideon fell silent.

"What are you up to tonight then?" Eddie thought he'd better fill the awkward silence. He almost heard Gideon shrug through the phone.

"Not much. I'm lying down flicking through TV channels, debating whether to go back downstairs and catch up on some paperwork. What are you doing?"

"I'm about to have dinner with my housemates. One of them cooked this whole pasta thing. I just got out of the shower."

"Out of the shower, hey?" Gideon's voice sounded much more interested in that titbit. "What, so you're naked then?"

Eddie's chest thumped and his cock slowly tented the towel. "Not quite. I'm in a towel." His hand moved slowly down to caress himself through the fabric of the thin bath sheet. He couldn't help a slight gasp escaping his lips as he did so. On the other side of the phone he heard the noise of someone moving around, the rustle of clothes or bed coverings.

"So you're all alone then?" Gideon's voice was husky and the sound of it sent a shiver through Eddie's body. He swallowed as he stroked himself.

"Yeah, it's just me and this rapidly rising problem I seem to have."

Gideon's chuckled stirred Eddie's cock harder and he couldn't help a slight moan as his hands brushed the tip and sent a surge of electricity through his groin.

"Are you doing what I think you're doing?" Gideon whispered down the phone. "Because if you are, it is so damned hot."

"I dunno. Are you doing something that side that *I* should know about?" Eddie stroked himself languorously as he lay back on the pillows, hugging his phone to his chin and ear and letting the towel fall to the side as he took himself in his hand. He was already wet and slick under his fingers, and just knowing Gideon was listening to him and knowing he was getting off was a complete turn-on.

"I'm lying naked on my bed, touching myself and wishing you were here to suck my dick. Then I could fuck you." Gideon's throaty growl made Eddie's buttocks clench together and he swore he felt the pressure of a cockhead at his entrance, so intense was the image of seeing Gideon behind him, ready to enter him.

"Crikey, you don't waste any time, do you?" he gasped, as his hands gripped firmer and he stroked harder at the thought of Gideon taking him.

"No time to waste," was the equally gasping retort. "Just thinking about bending you over and pushing inside you makes me want to come."

"Oh fuck." Eddie had no doubt if he saw himself in the mirror now, he'd see a wild-eyed, messy-haired man with pink cheeks and a purple cock, manically fisting himself as he tried desperately to make his sensations last.

Mental note: get a mirror installed so next time I do this I can watch. That would be bloody incredible. Better still, get Gideon here with me so we can watch ourselves rut like rabbits.

That idea made Eddie even hornier. He heard Gideon's low groans.

"God, Eddie, what you do to me. Want you, just can't stop thinking about you and that tight arse of yours… Want inside you so bad."

"Hell, you say the sexiest things." Eddie's legs tensed, his thighs straining with the effort of prolonging the orgasm that threatened. He didn't want to stop pumping his cock, yet at the same time, he wanted this experience to last longer. He was in agony deciding what to do. Finally he stopped his strokes and gripped the base of his shaft tightly as he tried to slow things down. "Tell me how you'd do it— how would you fuck me?"

Gideon's strangled voice gave confirmation the fact that he was in as delicate a place as Eddie. "I'd put you on your stomach, use my tongue and my fingers, eat your hole until you were ready, put my fingers inside you to open you up and then my dick would pound your gorgeous arse into the mattress."

Hearing those words, Eddie had no place to go but up. As his hands went back to their frenzied fisting of his cock, his balls drew up in his groin, his body stiffened like the onset of super rigour mortis and he cried out loudly as plumes of wet, warm semen shot out of him and covered his hand, wrist and stomach with come.

Eddie chanted, "Oh God, oh God," over and over again like a prayer. The phone fell onto the bed and he scrambled to pick it up desperately, not wanting to miss the sounds of Gideon's climax. He pressed the phone back to his ear with shaking hands as his still-shuddering body collapsed back on the bed.

There was a loud explosion of noise over the phone, something that sounded like a cross between a roar and a snort and he heard Gideon moaning softly, words he couldn't make out. Eddie listened for a while and then when his heart had finally calmed down and he could breathe properly again he spoke into the phone.

"G? You there?"

There was a shuffling noise and then Gideon's deep voice resonated down the phone, breathy and relaxed. "Yeah, I'm here. Hell, that was something. I haven't come like that in ages. Nearly blew my damn balls off."

Eddie felt a sense of pride in being able to engineer such a response. "Well, let me tell you, it was pretty explosive this side too. Now I have to have another shower or the proboscis downstairs will be all over me."

"Proboscis?" Gideon sounded out of breath.

"My flatmate can smell something at a thousand paces. He's the Svengali of scents."

"Oh. I see."

Eddie felt a prickle of unease at the suddenly flat tone of Gideon's voice. He mentally kicked himself for bringing up the sensitive subject of smell. He babbled on.

"Anyway, that was a lot of fun. Pity you weren't here so we can act out some of those fantasies you have."

"I'd like that." The smile was back in Gideon's voice. "If you didn't have plans with your housemates, I'd ask you to get your butt over here so we could do that." His voice was hopeful and Eddie sighed in disappointment.

"I'd love to, but after the attack the other night, Leslie's on this whole mother-hen thing and he's cooked and we're waiting for Taylor to get home so we can relax together. I can't let them down."

"I understand. No problem then." There was silence. Eddie wondered what the right thing was to say to your boss after you'd given him a blow job then had phone sex with him. He didn't think *that* would be in the *Dummies, Get your Boss to Like You* book, should such a thing exist. He bit back a chuckle.

"Uhmm, I checked your shift schedule earlier and you're off tomorrow night it looks like. Do you want to go out with me, watch a film or something?" Gideon sounded shy, unsure and Eddie's heart melted.

Gideon actually checked my schedule?

"Yeah, sure. We can go watch that new Spider-Man movie if you like?"

Hell, way to tell the man I'm a dork and a geek. Spider-Man, for God's sake. I could have chosen something a little more cerebral like one of those highbrow independent films at the Ritzy.

"Spider-Man sounds good. I like super hero films. Great escapism."

Eddie was relieved Gideon was apparently as big a geek as he was. "Okay. That's a date then." Eddie squirmed. A date? Was that what it was?

Gideon gave a quiet laugh. "Yeah, it's a date. I'll see you around tomorrow anyway, but tomorrow night is ours."

"Cool. I'll see you tomorrow then."

"Eddie?"

"Yes?"

"Are you really okay after that arsehole hurt you? Because if not, I have a baseball bat and I'm not afraid to use it to beat him to a pulp when he gets loose."

Eddie was touched by the concern in Gideon's tone. "I'm okay, honest. I'm a bit warier now than I was but that's probably a good thing, right? Being more careful when out and about."

"Just watch out for yourself. See you tomorrow." The line went dead and Eddie placed his phone on his bedside table with a smile. Then he gazed down at his belly and sighed heavily. It was definitely time for another shower.

*****

When he finally made it down to dinner it was to see Leslie and Taylor both seated in the kitchen, at the breakfast bar. Leslie raised one manicured eyebrow at him as he entered.

"Glad you could join us, honey. Two showers in one night? What gives?"

Eddie scowled. "Wow, nothing gets past you, does it?" He nodded at Taylor. "Hey there. You're looking tired, man. The business giving you the runaround?" He went over to one of the pots and dipped his finger in to sample the sauce. Leslie harrumphed loudly but made no move to stop him.

Taylor shifted on the bar stool. "It's been pretty busy with Greg not being there. The shop has been manic this week too, with all the festivals and promotions going on and people wanting to buy music and guitars and shit." His dark eyes were shadowed. "I haven't been sleeping all that well either. I think I need me some of Leslie's chamomile tea tonight." His long, coffee-coloured fingers twisted what looked like a set of rosary beads as he stared down at them with vacant eyes. He looked washed out, his normally warm brown eyes dull, his dark skin paler than usual. His face bore a haunted look.

Eddie walked over and clasped his shoulder gently. "You know if anything's worrying you, you have me and Leslie to talk to, right?" He decided to take the bull by the horns. "If there's anything weird going on in your life, like, you know, that psychic stuff you do, well, we might not understand it all but we can listen 'kay?"

Leslie nodded his head in fervent agreement. "Oh yes. You know I like to think of myself as quite a spiritual being, Taylor, so if there's anything you want to share, you go ahead."

Taylor smiled. "Thanks, guys. I know it must seem a little out there, me being like this and saying strange stuff sometimes, but I appreciate the concern. There's nothing anyone can do at the moment; it's just something I have to deal with myself."

Eddie noticed Taylor backtracked a little when he saw Leslie looking displeased at that comment.

"I mean, I know I have you two and you'll be the first ones I come to if I need to talk." He grinned, looking more like the old Taylor. "Maybe I just need to get laid. It's been a couple of days and the itch needs scratching."

Eddie raised an eyebrow. "I've heard stories about you and that music shop you work in. Sounds to me like there's no shortage of guys wanting to help you out in the storeroom or behind the alleyway." He had heard a few rumours about Taylor's propensity to casual jerk-offs and blow jobs, but the man never brought anyone home.

Taylor shrugged and grinned. "I never said I was a saint, Eddie. And I do work in the music industry after all." He chuckled. "Now what say we give this chicken dish Leslie cooked a go and see if it tastes as good as it smells?"

The trio were soon tucking into plates of steaming and very tasty chicken and pasta, and Eddie ate until he thought he would burst. He loved his time here at his home with these two men. He didn't think he could get better flatmates. He was only listening with half an ear when he heard the word "gingerbread." He flicked a glance to Taylor who was sitting deathly still, his eyes unfocused and his hands still in his lap. He kept muttering one word over and over again.

Gingerbread.

Leslie looked at Eddie, concern on his face.

"He's zoned out again," he murmured. "Another psychic guy I know said we should just leave him to get over it because if we interrupt him mid zone he could die. Or the spirit thingy that he's with could escape and roam our world forever."

Eddie glared at him. "Some comfort you are. That sounds like a lot of cock and bull to me."

Leslie shrugged. "'Swhat he said. So let's just clear up the dishes and maybe by the time we're finished he'll be back with us."

Eddie didn't like the idea of leaving Taylor in whatever world he currently inhabited but he didn't think they had a choice. Personally he still wasn't sure what the whole "psychic" thing was all about and it was outside of his comfort zone. But he'd been saved by it first-hand so he had to give it some value.

"So you had phone sex with your man, hey?" Leslie said casually as he washed the dishes and stacked them in the rack for Eddie to dry.

Eddie stared at him, feeling his face light up like a lighthouse beacon. "What?"

"I passed your room and couldn't help overhearing you." Leslie grinned. "It sounded like quite a session."

"You mean you stuck your ear to my door and listened," Eddie said acerbically. "My door was shut."

Leslie was unrepentant. "It's been a few days since I got any. I was in need myself and yours did just as good."

Eddie gazed at him in disbelief. "You wanked off to *me* jerking off? Hell, that's just not on."

Leslie flashed him a sly grin. "Live with it, girlfriend. You got yours, I got mine." He fluttered his eye lashes and mimed jerking off. "Oh God, oh God…" He laughed loudly as Eddie flushed scarlet and snapped the dishcloth at him. He dodged around the kitchen, trying to avoid Eddie's slaps and finally the two of them came to rest, out of breath, in front of the sink again. Eddie glanced at Taylor and saw him blink and take a deep breath. He went over and knelt beside him.

"Are you okay? You left us for a little while."

Taylor nodded, a dazed expression on his face. "Yeah, I'm okay." He looked around the room in apprehension. "I didn't do anything silly, did I? Sometimes I do funny things when I'm like that…"

"No," Eddie reassured his friend. "You just sat there and said the word gingerbread over and over again." His subconscious said he knew the significance of that word but for the life of him he couldn't recall why. "Taylor, are you sure you're okay when this happens?"

His friend gave a tight smile. "I've fucking lived with it all my life, Eddie. Well, since I was about five years old and can remember it. Believe me, I'm fine. This was mild compared to sometimes." A flash of pain shone in his eyes and Eddie wondered what else Taylor had seen when he was in his dream world.

"I don't remember much about this trance," Taylor murmured softly. "I just keep hearing some man saying stuff about gingerbread, and he sounds so lost and alone and scared. But I can't see him. But he knows you, Eddie." Taylor's voice strengthened. "And you know him. This is something to do with you. That's all I can get at this time."

Eddie's skin crawled with apprehension. He wasn't sure what the significance of it all was but he'd hazard a guess it wasn't anything good. His mother had a saying. "I feel it in my water, son," she'd say when she had an inkling something was wrong. And Eddie felt something in his water right now.

"Do you think it has something to do with that bloke who manhandled me the other day? Perhaps it's some sort of delayed reaction to that event…"

Taylor passed a hand over his eyes. "I don't know. I suppose it could be. But what the hell does gingerbread have to do with it?"

Eddie pursed his lips. "Perhaps the guy has an obsession with it," he said helpfully. "Maybe they'll get to his flat and find he has a shrine to gingerbread or something. Or maybe he kidnapped someone who was a baker and makes gingerbread houses." Again there was that flicker of something at the back of his mind that niggled at him.

Taylor snorted. "Oh that's funny," he smiled. "A shrine to gingerbread. I doubt that's it but it's a good story." Eddie was pleased he'd made Taylor feel a little better.

Leslie snickered at the conversation then pressed a cup of his "every solace known to man" chamomile tea into Taylor's hand. "Drink this," he commanded. "It'll do you good. Then we're going to watch *Priscilla* again and I want no arguments."

He flounced off and Eddie and Taylor looked at each other and groaned. They were about to be subject to *Priscilla Queen of the Desert*—again—and then no doubt *To Wong Fu* would follow. It was definitely time to have more than just a few beers and inure themselves against the charms of Terence Stamp and Patrick Swayze in drag.

Chapter 12

Gideon watched the closing credits of the Spider-Man film and winced. Sitting in these awful cinema seats really wasn't good for his back. He ached everywhere and needed to stretch his legs. He chewed his gum and looked over at Eddie who sat still clutching his nearly empty carton of popcorn and staring starstruck at the screen. The one thing Gideon did appreciate about his loss of smell was that his nostrils weren't assailed by the stench of popcorn. He hated the bloody stuff. Eddie, however, was a popcorn fiend and the carton he held was his second one.

"What a great movie," Eddie breathed reverently. "And there's something about a bloke in tight Lycra that really gets me going. But that Dane de Haan…" his voice trailed off and he looked at Gideon. "He's just gorgeous."

"Which one was he?" Gideon asked. He knew who played Spider-Man but that was the extent of his spidery senses.

Eddie stared at him wide eyed as he stood up, clutching his carton of popcorn to his chest as if he'd defend it with his life. "The guy who plays the Green Goblin."

"Oh." Gideon looked at Eddie curiously, feeling a pang of jealousy. "You like 'em cute and with floppy hair?"

Eddie grinned, put on his jacket then turned to walk down the stairs toward the exit. Gideon watched his backside contemplatively, wondering whether he'd be partaking of it later. He'd thought about kissing Eddie during the film but as they were in the middle of the seating and there were kids in the audience, he'd decided against offending anyone's sensibilities. It was definitely happening the minute he got him alone, though.

As they walked out, Eddie dropped his popcorn box into the bin and reached over to cup Gideon's face in cold hands. He kissed him long and hard right there on the steps of the cinema, causing Gideon to stand at immediate attention. He moved his gum to one side of his mouth and thought he really needed to think about giving it up now. It got in the way at awkward moments. Then Eddie released him.

"I like them cute and with floppy hair, yes. But I also like them all macho and growly with amazing lips and beautiful hazel eyes. I like them moody and difficult and challenging. Sound familiar?"

Gideon stared into mocking green eyes and lost his breath. He truly had no idea what it was about Eddie that affected him the way it did. He'd been with plenty of men in his time, but none had ever clutched at Gideon's heartstrings and made them sing the way Eddie did. He tried to keep it light.

"Well, if I find one of those, I'll be sure to send him your way. The only one around at the moment is a drop-dead sexy restaurant owner with a definite yen to ravage a young chef he knows."

Eddie's eyes darkened and Gideon could swear *he* growled. The sound sent a surge of electricity to his dick.

"Then I guess we'd better introduce them, see what happens." He leaned in and whispered in Gideon's ear. "I want to make out with you in a taxi, so damn the tube; we're taking an easy ride home. Call for one. The sooner the better."

Gideon nodded and found himself in the street hailing a taxi. He spat his gum into a rubbish bin and when a taxi stopped, they clambered in. Even before the directions back to Gideon's were given and the taxi had pulled off, Eddie's hands were burrowing under Gideon's jacket, under his lumberjack shirt and finding the bare skin of his ribs. Eddie's mouth nibbled at his ear and the side of his throat and Gideon found it difficult to breathe. That became even more of a trial when Eddie's mouth closed over his and Gideon was subjected to an exploration of his mouth that would have made a dentist squirm with its intimacy. Gideon was *so* definitely not calling the shots tonight. He wondered with a shiver if he ever would.

"You taste so good, of coffee and gum," Eddie murmured as his tongue slid into Gideon's ear. "You're forever chewing that stuff. Don't you ever get tired of it? Doesn't your jaw ache?"

"The only time my jaw will be aching will be when I'm sucking you off," Gideon managed to gasp out between kisses. Eddie's body trembled in his arms and his kisses became even fiercer. Gideon saw the taxi man regarding them in the rearview mirror and he hoped the guy was tolerant of men making out in his vehicle.

It was all he could do to scrabble around in his pockets and find the money he needed to pay the man when they reached his flat. Eddie's hands were still all over him and Gideon felt quite faint. At this rate he didn't think he'd make it upstairs to the bedroom. Visions of bending Eddie over the buffet counter sprung to mind and he groaned.

Unhygienic, a potential Health and Safety fine of alarming proportions and so not what I want tonight to be about. I don't want fumbling in the office or stolen kisses in a theatre complex. I want him in my warm bed, with the lights down low, soft sheets under our bodies and—oh my God, I want bloody romantic.

What the hell is all that about?

Finally they were inside the restaurant and Gideon was trying to pry Eddie's hands from his body.

"Eddie, I need to switch the alarm off. Or we'll have the damn security company around in a jiffy. Jesus, take your hands out of my pants so I can—for God's sake. Please let me punch the code in before you do that." His dick was rock hard in his pants and he shifted uncomfortably.

He was able to disarm the alarm despite the groping of his groin and he finally managed to get space between him and Eddie. "Right. Let's go upstairs and take a deep breath so I can think and not blow a gasket before we even get properly busy. Maybe have a drink first." He cast a wry glance at an unabashed Eddie. "You are not good for my sanity, you know that?"

He propelled Eddie ahead of him across the restaurant and up the stairs to his flat. He armed the alarm again, forever hopeful he wouldn't have to disarm it later if Eddie decided to leave. Gideon had hoped that he would stay the night, wake up with him in the morning rather than disappear once the evening was done.

He opened the door and pushed Eddie inside. "You've been here before so I imagine you know where everything is—kitchen, bathroom. Do you want a drink? I have wine, beer, vodka…"

Eddie nodded. "Vodka and Coke please."

Gideon grimaced at that choice. Eddie followed him into his compact open plan kitchen, and then made Eddie his drink. He filled it with ice, gave it to Eddie and opened the tab to his beer.

Eddie grinned at him wickedly. "Dine me, wine me then fuck me? Is that the plan for tonight, G?"

Just the mere thought of being inside Eddie, having him beneath him on his bed, surrounded by his heat and with his mouth on his, caused Gideon to shiver and his dick to strain against the zipper of his jeans. He was so ready to have this man in his bed and if truth be told, in his life.

That thought scared the shit out of him.

Gideon was all too aware just how fast he was falling. He put his beer down on the kitchen counter, and took Eddie's drink from his hand. Eddie's lips were parted slightly, his eyes darkened and his gaze focused on Gideon's face. He swallowed and Gideon saw his Adam's apple bob up and down.

"You are a damned tease," he murmured softly as his hands framed Eddie's face, the slight feel of stubble under his fingers an aphrodisiac. He leaned in and pressed his lips to Eddie's, and the sound that came out of Eddie's mouth was the most erotic thing Gideon had ever heard. It flooded his senses with want.

"You need to get undressed," he growled as his hands began ripping Eddie's shirt from his shoulders. All thoughts of the calm before the storm had ceased. "I want you naked on my bed, right fucking now."

Eddie's lithe frame was a portrait of decadence as Gideon set to the task of stripping him. His body was taut lines, muscles that rippled beneath the surface of pale, freckled skin the colour of cream and just as smooth. It was hidden curves and crevices, and the V-line of his hips made Gideon's mouth water. He wanted to lick it, feel that skin beneath his lips. He might not be able to taste the man but by God he could feel him. Feel that warmth and desire that was causing Eddie's breath to get deeper with each uncovering of his body. Finally Gideon had him naked in front of him; Eddie's long, thick prick was swollen, already wet. It was a work of pure art. Gideon reached out a finger and dipped a tip into the slit, scooping up the wetness there and then raised it to his lips. It was warm, thick and for a brief moment he despaired that he couldn't taste anything of the man that was Eddie Tripp. Then he lost all sense of reason as the man who had Gideon in knots reached down and released Gideon's own needy prick into his warm hands.

"God, that feels good," Gideon managed to get out of a throat that was clogged with desire. "I wish I could smell you. I don't even know what you taste like." He heard the yearning in his voice and felt the tug at his chest.

Eddie moved forward and ran a hand across Gideon's jaw, his fingers warm and calloused. "You can feel me, and hear me, G," he whispered back as his hands undid Gideon's trousers and he began the task of undressing him. "Every bit of me is yours. There's no place you can't go, nothing you can't do to me."

Gideon's breath hitched at those words, his heart beating faster. Eddie pushed Gideon's trousers and briefs down his hips and they fell to his ankles. He stepped out of them as Eddie then pulled his shirt over his head. Gideon was naked now and Eddie stepped back to look at him, his nostrils flaring, his eyes darkened with desire. "And look at you. You're gorgeous. Just perfect."

He trailed his hands down Gideon's hips, brushed them against his hairy thighs, and Eddie's wrist fleetingly brushed his prick. Gideon hissed and closed his eyes in pleasure.

Eddie carried on with his words of torture. "I love the hair on your body. I want to run my fingers through it, taste it. I want to take your cock in my mouth and suck you, feel you come. Then I want you inside me, need you there. I need you to fuck me, G."

Gideon could take no more of the erotic talk. His cock was straining upward, his balls felt as if they were going to burst with the power of Eddie's words alone. Green eyes met dusky brown and Gideon pulled Eddie to him in a fierce embrace and took his mouth with all the feeling he had inside him.

Eddie moaned against his lips as Gideon all but pushed him through to his bedroom. The beside-the-bed lights threw off a soft, warm glow, shadowing the walls with their entwined figures, an erotic display of male need and strength. Gideon threw Eddie onto the bed as Eddie chuckled sexily, the sound targeting Gideon's cock like sonar.

Eddie lay back on the cotton duvet, his hands moving up over his head as he licked his lips and looked up at Gideon standing by the bed. Eddie spread his legs wide and Gideon felt dizzy at the delicacy now being displayed just for him. The man before him looked like a decadent red-headed, cream-skinned angel, his tight bum cheeks, that rosy, puckered hole and the thatch of reddish-blond hair between his legs taunting Gideon.

"Is this what you want?" Eddie said teasingly. He moved one hand and dragged it lightly down his cock. "Or this?" He moved his finger suggestively down toward his arse and Gideon growled as he leapt onto the bed and stilled the man's hand, clenching it tightly in his own.

"Christ, how does someone that looks like an angel manage to sound so damn dirty and sexy?" He shifted to kneel beside the man splayed before him. "You know you drive me crazy, right? Totally, batshit crazy." Gideon pulled Eddie to him and once again, the two men's bodies merged, cocks rubbing together, skin to skin, both desperately seeking the other's touch. Hot tongues slicked against each other, teeth grazing lips, mewls of satisfaction echoing from both of their lips as they rolled and tussled on the bed, sweat and semen holding them together like the glue of sex.

*****

Eddie was lost in the sensation of having Gideon's tongue in his mouth, his lips against his, his body pressing him into the bed as if he wanted to imprint him into the very fabric itself. Eddie wasn't generally a really dirty talker in bed, but Gideon brought out the wild animal in him, the side that said to hell with everything and let this man take him with all the energy and power that he had. His arsehole was actually clenching at the thought and all he could think of was having that steely rod of flesh inside him, pounding him hard until he came, and nothing else was going to assuage that burning need he had. If Eddie was the angel, Gideon was the devil, his hard, masculine body the torment, and the only release would be having the pleasure of being finally fucked by the man he'd desired for a long time.

Eddie cried out softly as Gideon's fingers found his hole and caressed the skin around it. He pushed himself toward Gideon's seeking fingers and Gideon laughed quietly.

"Steady on, tiger. Let me at least get you a little lubed up. I don't intend going in dry." Nimble fingers stroked at Eddie's entrance, sunk deep down inside him until he wanted to scream from the pleasure of the feeling. He closed his eyes, revelling in the scent and taste of the man on top of him, hearing his soft sighs and grunts, and when he heard the rip of the condom packet Eddie nearly came undone. Soft light flooded behind his eyelids as he gasped at feeling Gideon seat himself at his hole, pushing tentatively. Yet Eddie could feel Gideon's restrained urge to plunge inside him in the tautness of his biceps as Eddie hung on for the ride.

"Okay there?" was the whispered entreaty in his ear and Eddie shivered as he pushed his hips toward Gideon's, the need to merge with this man a primal instinct.

"Just do it," Eddie gasped as he clutched at Gideon's arse and propelled him deeper inside. "Please, G. Need to feel you more. Oh my God…" his words were cut off by the deep intake of air he took as Gideon pushed fully inside him, hot silk and steel forged together to make a weapon Eddie wanted to feel pierce him deeper and harder. Their lips clung together, tongues greedy and grasping as both men moved together, bodies synchronised like athletes at their prime, slick, rhythmic movements that would no doubt have won gold at the Olympics. In between air breaks, Gideon's breathing was harsh, his warm, peppermint-and-coffee-fragranced breath like a soft caress against Eddie's cheek.

"God, you feel so dammed good," Gideon whispered, "I feel like I could live inside you, you know that? You were made for my cock."

Eddie chuckled in between finding his breath. "You say the sweetest things. I like having you home."

The soft laughter that rumbled through Gideon's chest made Eddie flush with heat and pleasure. It had been too long since he had heard this man sound happy. The sensation of flying and dizziness assailed Eddie's brain as he gasped, feeling his own climax building. The rub of his cock against Gideon's hard belly seemed to be all he needed to release the pressure he felt building his balls. Just to make sure, he reached down and stroked himself.

Oh yes, I am definitely there. That feels so good…

"I am so ready…" Gideon grunted and Eddie fisted himself faster as his head swum and his body tensed, his balls pulling up as he came, hot semen spurting from the end of his dick to splatter between the two bodies that were slick with sweat and fluids. His cry of triumph as he arched up and tightened himself around Gideon's cock was obviously all it took for Gideon to throw back his head, his neck muscles corded tightly, and let out a loud groan of ecstasy as he climaxed. Eddie's body still shuddered with the aftershocks of his orgasm and from the slight tremors rocking Gideon's body, he felt the same. Finally Gideon collapsed on top of him, nuzzling Eddie's sweaty neck and slowly licking a trail from his jawline to his ear. Gideon seemed to have fascination with his ears, a part of himself Eddie had never really liked because he thought they were too big. Eddie's cock stirred and Gideon groaned.

Eddie grinned. "I'm younger than you, remember? My cock doesn't take much encouragement to get hard. So maybe you should stop that and get that off me so you can recover, old man." He waited with bated breath for Gideon's reaction to his teasing.

Gideon pushed himself up over Eddie, his eyes indignant as he opened his mouth to say something biting. Then he smiled down at Eddie and leaned down and kissed him tenderly.

"You little bastard. I see the way things are. You're going to give me hell, aren't you?" He leveraged himself to the side of the bed onto his back, pulling off the spent condom and dropping it beside the bed. They lay there, chests still heaving, staring up at the ceiling. Eddie wasn't sure whether to move over and cuddle or stay his side of the bed. He had no idea—now that the urge for each other had been fulfilled—whether this was simply a one-off and he needed to leave, or whether he was welcome to stay. He knew which one he wanted.

His decision was made for him as Gideon reached out and drew him closer, into his shoulder, so that Eddie's head was on Gideon's chest.

"Sleep," he said gruffly as he pulled the covers around them. "We can get up early and clean up, take a shower. I hope you don't bloody snore. That's a deal breaker."

Eddie snuggled into his lover's broad chest, his heart leaping at the fact he wasn't being kicked out. "I might, a little. I hope you don't fart. *That's* a definite deal breaker."

Gideon's low chuckle reverberated against Eddie's cheek. "Everybody farts in bed, sunshine. This isn't a romance novel."

Eddie's nose twitched. "Well, at last give a man some warning so he can hold his breath." His eyes closed as the steady thrum of Gideon's heartbeat in his ear. "And no molesting me when I sleep. I want to be awake for anything you want to do me." He looked up at Gideon with a leer and a hopeful glance.

"Oh you'll be awake," Gideon agreed quietly, his eyes soft and Eddie flushed with heat at the need in those eyes. "I'm no necrophiliac. I want my prey to be alive and kicking when I molest them."

"Good," Eddie murmured sleepily, already half asleep. "I guess that's our list of demands done then. Now let's get some shut eye. You wore me out."

As he slipped into the warm darkness of slumber, he heard Gideon's soft words, said with affection.

"There's plenty more where that came from."

Eddie fell asleep with a smile on his face knowing there were more nights like tonight to come.

Chapter 13

Eddie was on cloud nine for the next two weeks. He floated through the kitchen at work, leaving himself open to taunts and teasing from his fellow workers about the constant smile on his face and how it got there. He and Gideon saw each other often and it was no secret at the restaurant. Eddie had thought Gideon would be closed-mouthed about their relationship but instead, the man seemed to be proud of the fact he was bedding Eddie.

He took his staff's good-natured ribbing in his stride and grinned when they made ribald comments. Eddie also melted each time Gideon's eyes met his across the kitchen—a place he'd taken to coming more often that he had in the past. Those smouldering, possessive glances had led to bedroom calisthenics most nights in Gideon's flat and Eddie was definitely feeling well exercised.

The euphoria ended Wednesday midday when he came in to work a half-hour early for his shift and found the restaurant in an uproar. It wasn't opening time yet, but staff were anxiously scurrying about, avoiding conversation, seemingly harassed. As he walked in, he saw quick glances darted in his direction and tight smiles. Perturbed, he went to Gideon's office to see what was going on. The door was locked. He listened and heard the faint low sound of someone talking inside. He knocked.

"G, are you in there?" He sniffed. There was the faint smell of burning plastic and something else lingering in the air. Smoke and something chemical.

There was no reply to his question so he tried again. "Why is the door locked? Is everything all right?"

"Just go away, Eddie. I'm fine." The fierce growl from behind the door certainly didn't give Eddie any confidence that things were all right or that Gideon was fine.

"What's going on?" He knocked again, louder this time. "Gideon, for God's sake let me in."

"Go away!" was the shouted retort. "I'm not in the mood for company right now. Just leave me the hell alone."

Eddie's throat constricted and he swallowed.

He won't even talk to me? What the hell is wrong with him? I thought…

His thoughts tailed off. Yes, he'd thought perhaps they were a bit more than they were, not just fuck buddies, but perhaps that had all been a mistake.

Perhaps I read too much into this whole thing. Fuck. I always do this. I always get too close and get hurt.

He remembered Simon. He had pissed off and left as soon as Eddie started mentioning going on holiday together. And Lewis— he'd point-blank laughed in his face and told him that he was just a "pleasant distraction" as he went back to his older boyfriend. Eddie knew he was probably overreacting, but given the state of his past love life, he thought he had the right to feel a little paranoid.

A gentle hand on his shoulder made him start and he turned in surprise to see Carmen smiling at him in sympathy.

"Eddie, come on. You know there's no use talking to him in this mood. I had hoped as it was you…" she sighed deeply. "Never mind. Come get a coffee and I'll fill you in. It's been a bloody nightmare this morning."

Eddie stole one more glance at the locked door. "Please talk to me, Gideon," he pleaded but there was no response. His heart heavy, he followed Carmen into her office where she had her own coffee machine. He perched his backside on the corner of Carmen's small desk as she busied herself with making drinks. She made him a latte with the coffee pods and handed it to him.

"There you go." She made her own then sat down in her rather wonky typist's chair and looked at Eddie.

"This morning, that bloody printer on the table behind Gideon's desk shorted out. It's an old damn thing and I've been trying to get him to replace it for ages. It shocked him the one time but he said he'd fixed it." She made a moue. "Apparently not. There must have been some faulty wiring. Gideon was sitting in his office reading some financial accounts. The whole thing burst into flames and was merrily burning away. He didn't smell a thing. It was a bit like a repeat of the whole kitchen dishtowel episode, but worse. It was only Andy coming past his office to get to his shift and smelling the fucking thing that alerted anyone. There wasn't so much smoke then. He rushed in and alerted Gideon and then found the fire extinguisher. The darned thing was blazing away by then. He managed to put out the fire."

Eddie's heart sank at Carmen's story. He knew Gideon would not have taken the event lightly.

"What happened then?" he asked softly. "Isn't there a smoke detector in his office?"

Carmen shrugged her shoulders. "It didn't go off. Then Gideon lost it. He was ranting and raving about how he could have burned down his restaurant and killed everyone. We tried to tell him that wouldn't have happened but he wouldn't listen. Stubborn bastard." Her eyes darkened. "He went bat shit is more like it. He threw what was left of the printer against the wall, kicked his chair over and shoved everything off his desk, including his PC." Her voice faltered. "Then in front of everyone he had a panic attack."

Eddie closed his eyes in regret. His proud lover would not have taken kindly to everyone seeing him have a meltdown.

Carmen carried on in a slightly shaking voice. "I managed to get him settled but it was bloody scary seeing him like that. Hyperventilating, as white as a sheet and then he blacked out. I've seen it before but never that bad."

Eddie reached over and took her cold hand. "They can be pretty frightening to watch. My mum has them, so I know." He took a deep sigh. "So now my stupid boyfriend has locked himself in his office and refuses to talk to anyone? Figures."

Carmen smiled slightly. "Boyfriend? Does Gideon know that?"

Eddie flushed. He'd shot his mouth off too soon. The term had just slipped out. It was how he thought of Gideon, though. They hadn't just shared sex; they'd been to films, dinner, a concert or two and even taken a sail down the Thames on a dinner boat. He'd liked the idea of calling him boyfriend but he wasn't sure how Gideon felt about it.

"It's better than *fuck buddy*." He rolled his eyes. "And no, G doesn't know I use that term around him and don't you tell him. I don't want to scare him off forever."

"You really like him, don't you?" Carmen said gently as she sipped her coffee. "He likes you too, I can see. I've never seen him with anyone else like he is with you."

"Yeah, well." Eddie felt a lump in his throat despite Carmen's words. "He told me to leave him the hell alone; he doesn't want to talk to anyone. I don't know where that leaves me."

Carmen squeezed his hand. "He'll come around soon. We just need to let him simmer down." Her face was worried. "He really needs to talk to someone about the attacks and his moods. I thought he was going to see someone after the last conversation I had with him, but that doesn't seem to have happened." Her face lit up. "You need to talk to him about it too."

Eddie sighed gloomily. "I have. I've been a real pest, trying to push him into it over the past few weeks. I even went so far as to call my doctor and get a card for a recommended therapist. Gideon said he'd call him but I don't think he has yet. He has these nightmares and wakes up in a cold sweat. I think I'm slowly convincing him to get help; he just has to take that first step." Eddie loved sleeping with Gideon in his bed but the occasional nightmares were something else. "We talk about it a little more now though which is a good sign. So he's caving slowly to pressure. I just hope he comes around soon before he bursts a blood vessel."

*****

Gideon sat behind his desk in his locked office, his hands tapping out an agitated tattoo on his desk. He'd managed to salvage most of the items he'd swept off it in his temper earlier but his PC was never going to work again. It was irrevocably screwed. He'd kicked it into the corner intending to take it to the local recycling centre and he supposed he'd have to buy a new one now. He scowled fiercely. *And a new fucking printer.* Andy had been diplomatic enough to remove the offensive item from his office after putting out the fire. It was just as well, as Gideon thought he'd still be kicking the crap out of it.

He stared moodily into space, chewing his gum as he'd really craved a smoke, and trying to ignore the guilt sitting heavily in his chest at sending Eddie away. He'd heard the hurt in his voice as he'd pleaded with Gideon to talk to him.

I just can't yet, he thought desperately. *I need to get this blackness out of me, let it drain away like oil-stained water. I'm no use to you like this.*

Gideon had no doubt that his feelings for Eddie, even in just such a short time, were not simply a matter of lust. Eddie was peace to Gideon's war, his warmth to Gideon's chill. Even Rafael hadn't come this close. Gideon realised that now. Eddie was funny, quirky, cute, and when he was in the sack, he was a different person. Demanding, aggressive and so damn sexy. Someone Gideon was falling in love with. That was why he needed a little space right now.

He was also ashamed to admit that he was envious of Eddie in the kitchen. He'd spent more time in there the past two weeks. Seeing Eddie's skills and his incredible ability to create dishes that Gideon thought looked sublime had highlighted Gideon's own insecurities about no longer being what he was. He'd received a phone call earlier today–before the printer episode—from a mainstream newspaper wanting to feature Eddie in their "Culinary London" insert special as their featured chef. Of course Gideon had said yes—not only was it good for Eddie's career it was good for Galileo's as well—but it still rankled. That should have been him in the papers. Thinking like that shamed him deeply.

Lost in his thoughts, he didn't notice someone standing before him. He looked up, startled, into a sea of emerald green that regarded him evenly. His temper flared.

"How did you get in?" he demanded as he stood up to face Eddie. He glanced at the open door.

"Jerome helped. Apparently this office used to be a large storeroom and he still has a key." Eddie moved around closer to Gideon. "Please don't give him any grief. We were all worried about you."

Gideon noticed Eddie seemed hesitant to touch him and his heart tightened.

Was that what it's come to? He feels he can't touch me in case I have a hissy fit?

"Very MacGyver-like of you," Gideon said quietly.

Eddie turned back and closed the door. "Do you want to talk about it?" He regarded Gideon with both affection and a little wariness.

Gideon shook his head. "I'm sure you've heard everything there is to hear from Carmen or Andy or anyone else that happened to see the sorry event of this morning." His tone was scathing.

Eddie's face darkened. "Gideon. It happened. There's really no need to get all bent out of shape over it. Luckily someone smelt it and got it under control…" His voice tailed off and he stared at Gideon uncertainly.

Gideon felt the shame and frustration building in his chest and stomach and he fisted his hands. "So it's no big deal, is it? The fact I couldn't smell burning behind me which could have led to me torching this place, myself and let's not forget the other people in this building? The fact that the smoke detector that I only had tested about a week ago and was working fine *didn't* work because of whatever fucking reason—who knows with those bloody things. I think that's a pretty big deal, Eddie." He was close to shouting now in his agitation.

Eddie's eyes widened. "Calm down. You don't need another panic attack—"

Gideon saw Eddie clamp his lips shut and a look of chagrin cross his face. He seemed to realise he'd poked the bear for a second time. Gideon leapt on that bandwagon like a trumpeter playing a march for an approaching army.

"Oh and of course then I have to go all *emo* and have an attack that everyone in here saw and Carmen had to help calm me down. Just the sort of thing an employer needs his employees to see." His chest heaving, Gideon kicked the piece of debris on the floor that still remained as evidence of his transgression. It looked like part of his computer.

"Oh for Christ's sake, you're a fucking human being. No one thinks any less of you for what happened or for you having thrown a bit of a wobbly." Eddie's voice was heated. "The only person blaming himself here is you. And perhaps if you'd talked to someone professional about what happened to you in that fire six months ago, you'd be dealing with things better."

Gideon stared at the flushed face of his lover, at the glittering green eyes staring back at him with passion and a little trepidation, perhaps at being so bold.

The gauntlet had been thrown and it was up to Gideon to pick it up. He moved closer to Eddie, invading his personal space, and Eddie's nostrils flared. He leaned into Eddie's face and spat the words he wanted to say out. "Have you ever smelt someone burning to death? Ever had a smouldering beam fall on you, pinning you to the floor while your skin scorched?"

Eddie's face whitened but to his credit he held his ground, staring at Gideon's face like a man seeking a revelation. "Hugh might have been dead when the wall fell on him and cracked his skull wide open, but he was on fire." Gideon's voice was hoarse as he recalled the event of that night. He'd never said this to anyone before. "I couldn't get to him, I wasn't even *sure* he was already dead at that point. I thought he had to be because he wasn't screaming while he burnt. But someone *was* screaming and that someone was me. I screamed for someone to help him, to stop him charcoaling like some sort of pig roast at a BBQ." Gideon's chest was heaving now, his voice stuttered and heavy. "Eventually I couldn't scream anymore because of the smoke."

Eddie reached out to touch his shoulder and Gideon shook it off. The wounded expression in Eddie's eyes cut Gideon to the core but he was on a roll now. All the things he'd never said to anyone came vomiting out of him like a kid on a fairground ride who'd eaten too much cotton candy. "All I could feel was the pain in my side as I burnt, and hear the crackling of his flesh as it cooked. It's true you know. It sounds just like a roast in the oven, spitting and sizzling. Smells like it too." Gideon felt his face contort with remembered disgust at the overwhelming smell of cooked meat.

Eddie's face was a mask of horror and despair. He opened his mouth to speak but Gideon put a strong hand over his mouth. "This is my turn to speak. You want me to share? This is me sharing while you shut up."

Eddie took a step back and his hand grabbed at the desk as if looking for support. His face was milk white, his lips trembled and his eyes resembled someone who'd seen something from a nightmare. They showed dark, deep depths of pain and regret for Gideon.

"I was the lucky one. My burns were only second degree because they got to me in plenty of time. But Hugh looked like one of those crispy critters you see in CSI, all scrunched up and black and red." His head swum with the visions of Hugh's horribly mutilated body. "The firemen were there very quickly, thank God. They managed to get me out before the smoke got to me too much or the flames did too much damage. I woke up in hospital looking like a fucking mummy, with bandages everywhere." He shuddered at the memory of that pain. "But I was the lucky one, I recovered well. And then I discovered I'd lost the ability to smell anything. I can't even distinguish between salty and sweet like some people can. Nothing. " His voice faltered. It was strange how that little fact had been the proverbial straw that broke the camel's back. A man was dead; Gideon had been grievously injured; yet this singular fact and the loss of what he saw as his passion for his culinary art had broken him.

A wave of dizziness swept over him and he passed a hand over his eyes, rubbing at them like a child. Eddie moved forward, his face determined, and strong arms encircled Gideon as he pulled him into a ferocious embrace. Gideon tried to pull away but Eddie wasn't having it.

"Fucking let me hold you, G," he snarled. "You need me, you arsehole. You know you do. Stop fighting me."

Gideon *did* need Eddie's strength. He needed Eddie's arms around him, keeping him safe and grounded. He wanted Eddie's voice in his ear, his breath on his mouth, his skin against his. He just simply wanted Eddie. He sunk into Eddie's hard body, collapsing like a black hole as his arms slid around his lover's waist and he clung on like a drowning mouse to a reed.

All the frustrations he'd held in for so long, all the pain and disappointments, all the fear and self-hatred flooded to the surface and the floodgates opened as Gideon cried hot tears. Eddie's deep voice in his ear soothed him, murmured words of support and affection. Gideon wept for his dead friend, for the loss of his calling, for the nights spent waking up covered in sweat as he relived the event. Finally he was spent and he remained plastered against Eddie's broad chest, while strong hands stroked his back and hair and told him everything was going to be all right.

And for once, Gideon believed that it might be so.

He sniffed, hiccupped and finally loosened himself from Eddie's hold to rummage in his desk drawer for tissues. He wiped his eyes then blew his nose, wincing at the fact he sounded like a wheezing elephant. Eddie's eyes never left him. Gideon took a deep shuddering breath then gave a wan smile.

"Sorry you had to see that meltdown. I must look a mess."

Eddie's eyes shone with a teasing light. "Not to me. You look very dashing with your pink nose and cheeks."

Gideon scowled. "Idiot." But there was no heat in his tone. Instead he felt a growing love for the man who studied him now with such concern.

What if he doesn't feel the same? What if this is just temporary to him?

Eddie perched on the side of the desk, his long legs splayed out in front of him as he crossed his arms. "I have to ask. The fact you lost your sense of smell. Was that because you got trauma to the head?"

Gideon shook his head. "No. The doctors can find no physical cause. They say it's psychological, that I subconsciously block out smell because of what I smelt that night and my brain is protecting me from reliving it. They call it a conversion disorder." He shrugged. "Because my sense of smell is gone, so is my sense of taste. It's a common thing apparently."

Eddie stood up excitedly. "But that's great!"

Gideon frowned. "In what Eddie-universe is that news 'great'?"

"It means that if it's all in your head then maybe you can get it back. It means that there's hope."

Gideon stared at him. "You think I haven't tried? I stood in a kitchen once chopping garlic and onions, mixing curry pastes, using every spice and herb I could find, to try and electroshock my brain into smelling something again. I told myself I could, that nothing else mattered but getting that sense back. I've tried all manner of things to try and tell my damned head that I want to smell again but it's having none of it." He gave a defeated sigh. "The doctors say there is no magic way to do it. That one day I could simply wake up and it will be back as soon as my brain lets go of whatever is holding me back."

Eddie was still excited. "I still say it's hopeful. And there were a couple of things you didn't have back then that you have now."

"Oh yes?" Gideon knew the answer to one of them but wanted to hear Eddie say it. "And those are?"

Eddie moved forward and cupped Gideon's face. He laid his forehead against his. "One of them was the ability to talk about this whole thing and stop being so macho." He grinned. "The other thing is me."

"Now how did I know you were going to say that?" Gideon murmured as his lips brushed Eddie's.

Eddie smirked. "Well now that big stick up your arse is out, and you've shared your story with someone, maybe you can stop being so uptight. And perhaps then something good might happen." He stepped back from Gideon and narrowed his eyes. "I need you to promise me something. It's important to me."

Gideon heaved a sigh. He should have known Eddie would have demands. "Go on then. What am I to sign my soul away to now?"

"I want you to talk to someone professional, tell them what you just told me. They might help you more than you know."

"I was going to call—" Gideon's heated retort was cut off by a hard kiss from Eddie, a kiss that made his head reel and his dick swell.

"No negotiations," Eddie whispered against Gideon's mouth. "I won't ask for anything else. Just this one thing. Please, Gideon. It's just talking to someone."

Gideon heard the pleading in Eddie's tone and sighed. He knew it was way overdue and if it made Eddie happy...

"Fine," he grumbled." I'll do it. I still have that card you gave me, that guy in Enfield who specialises in this sort of thing. I'll give him a call."

Eddie's face lit up like a lighthouse beacon. "Really? Thank you, that means a lot to me."

Gideon laid a hand on Eddie's cheek. "*You* mean a lot to me," he muttered softly.

Christ, my big tough boss image has now been tarnished forever. This damn man has made me soft.

But the joy on Eddie's face at his promise was enough to light up the Taj Mahal and the moon at the same time. Gideon didn't think he'd ever been responsible for such a look of happiness on someone's face before. He found he liked the feeling and wanted to do it more often. For Eddie.

The sudden glint in Eddie's eyes and low growl that emanated from his throat should have warned Gideon what was about to happen. He found himself being propelled back against the scorched wall of his office and kissed to death. To be honest it wasn't a bad way to go, and the way in which he was being manhandled was doing wonderful things to his cock and his body; for a moment there he thought he'd already entered Nirvana. As a greedy, slippery tongue invaded his mouth and Gideon lost all sense of rational thought, he could swear he heard bells ringing.

The ringing bells unfortunately weren't some sort of "happy ever after" cartoon event but instead was Eddie's mobile.

Gideon wondered as he unglued his mouth from his lover's, why anyone would choose to have a tone that sounded like Gothic bells from a horror movie. Eddie moved away reluctantly and took his mobile from his jeans pocket.

"Sorry. That's my dad's ringtone. I need to get this one." He moved away and answered and Gideon busied himself with readjusting, trying to quell the rising erection in his pants into some sort of modicum of decency.

"Dad? Hi. How are things?" Eddie wandered around the room as he talked. Gideon watched him. Eddie frowned deeply.

"Really? Well you know Luke. He likes to have his alone time. Perhaps he's gone over to Greg's place or maybe Randy…oh, you've called them and he's not there?" His frown deepened. "Well, yeah, I'll try and give him a call. If he's ignoring everyone else, he'll probably take mine. You know how he is." He was quiet as he listened and Gideon saw the worried glance at him. "Well, I was intending coming home for Halloween in a couple of weeks' time. I got the time off already. I told Luke I'd see him then." Again he listened. Gideon sat down in his office chair and glanced at some paperwork. The prospect of stock and re-ordering didn't really take his fancy at this time and he sighed as he pushed it away.

Maybe I'll take the afternoon off. See if Eddie has time off and we can go watch movies and make out upstairs. Although I actually think he was due on shift five minutes ago. Jerome is going to damn kill me for making him late.

"Yeah, okay Dad. I'll try calling him. Speak later." Eddie hung up and stared at Gideon.

"It's my little cousin, Luke. He's seventeen and he's disappeared. No one's seen him since yesterday. I just need to make this call if it's okay?" He glanced at his watch and his eyes widened. "Shit! Then I'll need to get to work before Jerome comes in with a butcher's knife and slaughters the pair of us. You know what he's like with tardiness." He dialled a number.

Gideon did indeed know. He'd seen many an unfortunate victim of Jerome's wrath quiver in fear at the sight of the hulk-like chef storming upon them like the vengeance of Godzilla. It was sight that entertained him but one that he didn't want to be on the receiving end of—boss or not.

He nodded at Eddie. "Go ahead, make it quick. If he comes looking for you, I'll stall him off and protect your virtue." He grinned as Eddie fluttered his eyelashes at him girlishly.

"My hero," he simpered then stopped as someone obviously answered the phone on the other side. "Luke? What the fuck, mate. I've had my dad on the line asking me where you are and your mum is going crazy 'cause she didn't know where you were." His eyes narrowed. "Are you okay? You sound a bit funny. Have you been crying? Is everything all right?" His fierce protectiveness for his cousin entranced Gideon who not so long ago had been subject to it himself. "You have a cold? Okay…" His voice drawled off in uncertainty. "Where the hell are you, anyway, and why haven't you called your mum?"

There was a pause as Eddie listened and then scowled. "Well, okay then. Have fun. Just don't bloody do that again. It scares the living shit out of everyone and it's damn inconsiderate." He nodded at the phone. "Yeah, yeah. Just call her, okay? My battery is going flat and I have to go to work now so don't let me find out later that you didn't. And tell that mate of yours next time to have some sort of radio with him when he plans on going out on the river. You never know what can happen out there."

Gideon chuckled quietly at Eddie's parental tone and wondered idly if one day their kids might be hearing it. His heart lurched.

Jesus where the fuck did that *thought come from?*

"Well, I'll give you a call later when I get home. It will be a late one." He caught Gideon's eyes and winked. "Nah, I have something I need to do later with my boss. He's a damn slave driver and works me hard. Very hard. The man doesn't know the meaning of taking it easy. He's a real ball breaker."

Gideon's erection had been subsiding but now leapt to full mast again at the sly innuendo in Eddie's voice. Eddie gave him a cheerful but naughty grin. "Right, we'll speak later. And Luke, be careful with that cold. It's chilly out there on the water. Later, mate."

He put his phone back in his pocket and looked at Gideon. "He went off with a friend on a barge on the Broads yesterday and they apparently got stuck somewhere. He says he had no mobile reception and they've only just managed to get the boat started again and on their way home."

He didn't sound sure and Gideon raised an eyebrow. "You sound as if you don't believe him."

Eddie huffed. "He just sounded a bit weird. But then he always—"

The two of them jumped a foot when a loud bang echoed through the room and an angry voice belted out, "Eddie, you might be the boss' favourite but I need your arse in my kitchen right now! Don't make me come in and get you because you know I will!"

Jerome's Jamaican lilt always sounded more pronounced when he was pissed off, and Gideon hastily shooed Eddie toward the closed door.

"Get off with you before he comes in and beats the hell out of me and you both. He'll bitch-slap me just as much as he will you. He's no respecter of hierarchy when it comes to his kitchen."

Eddie leaned and stole a quick kiss. "I'll see you later then?"

"Count on it. Now go!" Gideon watched in apprehension as Eddie opened the door and slid past the man mountain standing outside it. Jerome's face was threatening but the wink he threw at Gideon made him feel better. Jerome just narrowly missed slapping the back of Eddie's head as he darted past, ducking as he did so. Jerome growled loudly.

"Eddie, my boy, you are playing with fire. Get your little arse to work right now before I have this man fire you."

Eddie's laughter echoed down the hall as he dashed away and Gideon acknowledged Jerome with a smile. The big man grinned at him warmly.

"Boss, everything okay?"

Gideon nodded. "More than okay, Jerome. Thanks."

Jerome nodded and Gideon noted the expression of satisfaction on his face when he next spoke. "That little tyke is good for you, I think. He makes you laugh and smile. It's been too long since I've seen that." He gave a wide smile and turned and disappeared in the direction of Eddie. Gideon laughed to himself.

Eddie was certainly that. The man had chipped away at the scars of Gideon's heart and found the living flesh beneath. Gideon would be forever thankful. He sat down at his desk and opened his desk drawer. He took out a small business card and sighed. He'd promised to talk to someone, so he might as well make the call now and get an appointment. He grinned. Eddie could show his appreciation for his efforts later. After all, Gideon thought he deserved a reward for doing what he was told.

*****

Three days later, Gideon beside him, Eddie sat in the waiting room of Martin Wingmore, the therapist recommended by one of Gideon's doctors. Eddie had insisted on accompanying him—firstly, to make sure Gideon actually went and secondly, as moral support for his lover. Gideon had not been convinced the appointment was a good idea, but Eddie had slowly chipped away all resistance. Personally, he thought Gideon had got so sick of all the constant hints over the past few weeks: the YouTube link videos in his inbox depicting stories of people who'd had therapy and "survived" and random *Keep Calm and Go to Therapy* posts on Gideon's Facebook wall. Eddie had made two posts which Gideon had promptly deleted with a frown. But the message had been received loud and clear.

Gideon fidgeted in his chair, looking nervous.

Eddie reached over and took his hand. "G, stop being so damn twitchy. All you're going to do is talk to the guy. He isn't going to bite you." His tone went lower. "I might do that, when we get home, if you're a good boy and take all your medicine…"

Gideon's eyes darkened and a pink tongue came out to lick his bottom lip. "Eddie, not here for God's sake. That's all I need, having a boner when I go in to see the psychologist."

His words were stern but his face was affectionate and his voice warm and like thick honey. When Gideon got turned on, his voice thickened and roughened.

"Much as I like that idea though, save it for later." He gave a quick glance around the waiting room, taking in the bookshelves and the leather furniture, the potted plants and abstract paintings on the walls.

Eddie was sure one of them was a picture of an elephant with an erection, with a dwarf riding on his back. Gideon had spluttered with laughter when Eddie had innocently blinked his eyes and imparted that little gem of wisdom. It had gone a long way to calming Gideon down though and he'd relaxed a little more after that.

Gideon started as the inner office door opened and a portly, bespectacled man with a kind smile appeared.

"Mr. Trent?" He stepped forward and held out a hand to Gideon. "I'm Martin Wingmore."

Gideon stood and shook his hand. "Pleased to meet you, Mr. Wingmore."

The man laughed. "Call me Martin, please. I'm pretty informal and seeing as how you're going to telling me some personal things about yourself, I think that's the best approach, don't you? Like friends although…not."

He grinned widely and Eddie warmed to him. He could see Gideon relaxing too. He stood up beside him, one hand resting loosely on Gideon's waist, the other entwined with Gideon's hand.

Martin extended his hand again and Eddie took it. "And you must be Eddie. I think I have you to thank for getting your man here, don't I? Gideon and I spoke a little while on the phone and I think your name might have been mentioned a couple of times."

Eddie felt a swell of pleasure that Gideon had told the man about him and that Gideon was considered "his man."

"His man" looked a little embarrassed at the conversation and Eddie chuckled. "I did sort of have to do some convincing but he's here now." Martin gestured to the door, indicating Gideon should enter his office.

Eddie squeezed Gideon's hand. "Go get 'em, tiger," he murmured softly. "I'll be waiting here when you come out." The look of gratitude and affection he got from those honey-coloured eyes made Eddie's heart bounce like a ping pong ball in his chest.

Gideon squeezed his hand back. "See you later." He followed Martin into the office and the door closed, leaving Eddie standing outside. He sighed and sat down, idly browsing through the magazines on the side table. Picking up one called *Psychology Today*, Eddie began reading while he waited for his lover to bear his soul.

Chapter 14

Eddie was woken very early in the morning by the steady sound of his mobile going off. He opened one eye sleepily, and saw Gideon's sleeping face only a few inches from his. He smiled softly and tried to extricate himself from the strong tug of Gideon's arms around his waist. The last week had been sheer bliss, going to sleep with this man and waking up in his arms. Eddie rather liked the fact that he appeared to be a sleeping balm for his lover. Not to mention the fact that he was getting regular sex.

Gideon had also made more appointments with Martin, once a week, and the arrangement seemed to agree with him. He and Eddie had talked a little about his first session and now Gideon seemed less troubled, more at ease with life. He'd even stopped chewing gum as much, saying he was more relaxed and didn't need it anymore.

Eddie was quite pleased, because as much as he appreciated Gideon giving up smoking, the taste of the nicotine gum didn't really turn him on. He preferred the taste of Gideon's mouth virgin and sweet.

Eddie had his own guilt to tackle, worrying about abandoning his housemates who hardly saw him anymore. The only saving grace were the regular pub nights when they all got together and either got drunk or talked about Leslie's current man squeeze.

Gideon muttered as Eddie got free and swung his legs over the side of the bed. He picked up his mobile off the charger and peered at it blearily. His spine chilled as he answered. At this time of the morning, three a.m., he didn't think it was good news.

"Leslie? Is everything okay?"

Leslie's voice babbled loudly in his ear. "No, it's not fucking okay. Taylor's gone all weird again and I can't get him to wake up. He's just sitting there in the hallway in his skivvies. Eddie, you have to come home, he keeps saying your name over and over again…" Leslie sounded frantic with worry and Eddie clambered off the bed and held the phone to his chin with his shoulder as he tried to pull on his jeans.

"Slow down, Leslie. Is he hurt, or just in one of his zone-out freaky things?"

"It's a fucking MAJOR zone-out freaky thing, Eddie." Leslie sounded like he was on the verge of crying. "He went to bed about midnight and I woke up when I thought I heard someone moving around. It was Taylor but he looked so damned scary, his eyes were all blank and he had this look on his face. Like he was possessed or something." Leslie's voice rose to a shriek. "Oh my God, you don't think he is, do you? Possessed like the chick from *The Ring*? Oh my God, Eddie what if something's going to come crawling along the top of the wall, oh Jesus, I can't cope with this." There was a wail on the other side of the phone and Eddie felt a shiver of fear run through his body at his friend's distress.

"Leslie? Are you still there? Tell me what the hell is happening. I'm on my way over there now."

By now Gideon was awake and looking at Eddie with concern.

"What's going on?" he said huskily.

"Leslie is freaking out because Taylor's had one of his fits." Eddie placed the phone down on the bed as he pulled on a tee shirt. The squawking noise from the phone continued and he grimaced as he picked it up again.

"Leslie, I'm on my way. Just hold out."

"Oh gawd, hurry up. I'll try and make it through until you get here. I need to get me some salt. Make it quick!"

The phone went dead. Eddie frowned at the cryptic salt comment as he threw his mobile on the bed as he finished getting dressed. Gideon looked puzzled as he sat up in bed, the sheet falling to his waist. Even in his worried state Eddie could appreciate the sight of broad shoulders and a tight stomach.

"Your roommate? What, is he having like, an epileptic fit?" Gideon swung onto his feet and began dragging on clothes.

Eddie looked at him. "What are you doing?"

"I'm going with you." Gideon's tone was firm. "There are no taxis, no tubes so you're going to need a car to get to Kennington at this time of this morning. And I happen to have one."

Eddie hadn't even known Gideon had a car. "Okay, thanks. I appreciate that." He thrust his feet into trainers, not even bothering to put on socks. In a few minutes they were both ready. Eddie tucked his phone into his jeans pocket and followed Gideon down the stairs as they made their way to the back entrance of the restaurant. Outside, the night air was cold and crisp.

"She's over here." Gideon walked over to small garage about fifty feet from the restaurant. Eddie had seen the building many times when he went to empty rubbish and shoo away drunks, but he'd never realised it belonged to Gideon. Gideon took out a bunch of keys and unlocked the steel roller door, pushing it up as his arms flexed and his biceps bulged. Another sight Eddie appreciated. The door was rusty and made a terrible groaning noise as it gradually opened to reveal a dark space. He could see the faint outline of a car.

Eddie stepped inside, squinting to try and see what it was. "How many times have you opened that damn door? It's like something out of a horror story, that noise." Something scuttled in the darkness and Eddie moved closer to Gideon.

Gideon shrugged. "The last time I had Ellie out was about two months ago when I went to Liverpool for a convention."

Eddie stared at him in disbelief. "You called your car Ellie?"

In the darkness Eddie saw the gleam of teeth. "After my mother. Ellie is a real lady. So was my mum."

Eddie hadn't ever heard Gideon mention his parents. He knew vaguely from Carmen that his father was still alive but off on some godforsaken mission somewhere as part of some organisation, but that was about it. Even Carmen knew very little. From the word "was," Eddie gathered Gideon's mother was dead.

"Oh. I'm sorry about your mum."

Gideon was quiet as he stumbled over to the wall and gave a small groan of relief. There was a click and then the garage flooded with bright light. Eddie winced as his eyeballs had self-ignited and then his jaw dropped. In the middle of the space, a sleek, cherry-red MX 5 Roadster Coupe sat gleaming. Eddie moved quickly toward the car and lovingly ran his hands over the hood.

"Oh, wow, Gideon. She's beautiful." He peered inside. "And automatic too. That must make her a bit special."

Gideon gave a loving glance towards his car. "Yes. I bought her about five months ago, just after the accident. I wanted an automatic because I'm a lazy git." He chuckled as he unlocked the car and it beeped. "Climb in. We have somewhere to be, don't we?"

Eddie needed no further invite. He opened the door, sat down and was soon inspecting the interior as Gideon strapped himself in.

"Seatbelt, Eddie, before we go anywhere." Gideon's admonishing tone made Eddie smile as he reached and clipped the belt across his chest. He fiddled with all the dials and the radio like a kid. He loved cars, but although he had a driver's licence, he'd never owned one. He'd driven his parents' cars if he needed to, as insurance and upkeep had been way too expensive for him to afford.

Gideon started the engine, which purred as if she'd only been driven yesterday, and he slowly reversed out of the garage, across the gravel drive and turned into the darkened street. Traffic was still fairly busy even at this time of night.

"Don't you want to shut the garage door?" Eddie asked in surprise. "Someone may steal something."

Gideon shrugged. "There's nothing in there worth stealing, only this baby." He patted the dash affectionately then leaned over and switched on the radio to Radio 1 and the bass sounds of dub step music filled the car. Not something Eddie was partial to but Gideon seemed to be enjoying it.

"So this friend of yours that's gone rogue. What's his story?" Gideon manoeuvred the little car through the streets with all the experience of a seasoned London driver. Aggressive, defensive and confident. Eddie found it a real turn-on and wondered if Gideon had ever made out in his car.

Well, there's always a first time if not.

Eddie didn't really want to get into the nitty-gritty of what Taylor was as he was sure Gideon wasn't particularly fanciful. He knew it would have to happen once they got to his house but perhaps he could postpone the explanation until then with a little dross.

"Leslie is a bit of a character, a real flamer and proud of it. He's a bit highly strung so just be wary when you see him. He might try to launch himself at you, wrap his legs around your waist, you know. He's very demonstrative."

Eddie giggled at the expression on Gideon's face. He didn't look particularly convinced of Leslie's good points. Leslie *was* an acquired taste, no doubt.

Gideon expertly moved the car around a slow-moving truck and sped down the road.

"Okayyy. What about zoned-out freak? The one who has the fits?"

Eddie blew out his cheeks. "Taylor has these…episodes." His voice trailed off and he cleared his throat.

Gideon glared at him in exasperation. "And? Is he on medication?"

Eddie sighed. "It's not the sort of thing you can take medication for." He fiddled with his seatbelt, aware of Gideon's rising impatience beside him. The car seemed to pick up speed and Eddie glanced at the speedometer. He was sure Gideon shouldn't be doing eighty miles an hour in the centre of London. The man was apparently something of a speed merchant.

Isn't he worried about speeding tickets?

"Fuck, Eddie, you're more evasive than a politician on Twenty Questions. What the hell's wrong with him then?" Gideon growled as he narrowly avoided hitting a rubbish bin on the side of the road. Eddie's backside clenched at that close call.

Oh, just cut to the chase before he kills us.

"Taylor is a psychic. He sees things. It's how he saved me when that bloke attacked me in the alley and he did the same for Leslie. He's the real deal. I've seen it myself."

A loud snort of disbelief and a bark of laughter was Gideon's response. "Oh come on. You believe in that shit?"

"Yes," Eddie said quietly as he stared at Gideon's profile. "I told you. He knew I was in trouble that night. There was no way he could see what was happening. Leslie was there too, for everything."

Gideon flashed a thoughtful look but didn't say anything. There was silence for a while and Eddie breathed a sigh of relief, hoping his friends were all right, when he saw they were only a few minutes away from his house.

"So Taylor saw this stuff happening to you and that's how you were rescued?" Gideon said. "I thought they came by and saw you."

Eddie felt a little uncomfortable. "No, that's not what went down. It's what we told the police because they'd never have believed us. If Taylor and Leslie hadn't come over when they did because Taylor had his vision, that guy would have stuck his cock in my mouth or worse." He shivered.

Gideon hissed a breath and his hands clenched angrily on the steering wheel. "Bastard. I still want to cut his nuts off for putting you through that."

Eddie reached out and ruffled his hair affectionately. "I like that you want to do that to him for me." He stopped and pointed. "That's my house on the corner, the one with the green door and the lights on. You can park behind that old Rover, that's Mr. Coolidge's parking and he's away in Thailand or something." He grimaced. "He likes the lady-boys. They go in and out of his flat all the time. He tried to get Leslie to visit him one time and Leslie slapped him with a piece of fish."

Gideon guffawed and Eddie laughed. "No, honestly. He was on his way home late with a piece of prime cod from Sainsbury's and Mr. Coolidge groped him. The man got slapped around the face with a wet fish for his troubles. He was not a very happy bunny."

Gideon and Eddie were both giggling now as Gideon pulled up and switched off the engine. Gideon held his sides as tears fell down his face. Eddie loved this side of him.

"I think I might like this Leslie of yours," Gideon spluttered. "Come on. Let's go see what's going on with your crazy friends."

Eddie stared at him as he got out of the car. "That's it? You're not going to give me any more grief over the whole visionary thing?"

Gideon came around the car and pulled him into a hug. "Babe, he saved you. Doesn't matter how but you say he did. That's all I need to know. I need to thank them both. Now come on. I want to meet this fish-slapping man and the mysterious psychic. "

Eddie didn't have to wait long. As if there was some rotating beacon on his head attracting drama queens, no sooner had he stepped onto the front porch and made to open the door than it opened from within and a bundle of long limbs and muscled flesh launched itself into his arms.

"Oh God, Eddie, thank God you're here. Taylor is so damn out of it and I just don't know what to do." Leslie's arms hugged him close as he buried his face in Eddie's shoulder. "Hmm, you smell nice. Is that Davidoff? You dog, you. Here you tell me you can't afford the good stuff—"

Eddie reached out a hand with difficulty as Leslie was squeezing him like a melon being fitted for a fruit salad. He was vaguely amused at the sight of Gideon watching with wide eyes as the hurricane that was Leslie latched himself onto Eddie like a leech.

"Leslie, sweetheart, calm down and focus. If you let me go, I can introduce you to Gideon and we can see what we can do to get Taylor sorted." With a testy huff of breath, Leslie released Eddie and swung his eyes slowly in Gideon's direction. Gideon flushed as

Leslie appraised him from top to bottom, with a definite focus on his package. Leslie licked his lips as he regarded Gideon's groin and Eddie choked back a laugh at Gideon's obvious discomfort at being so blatantly inspected.

"Well, Eddie, he's a bit of all right indeed. I can see why you got all bent out of shape when he—"

Eddie leaned forward and placed a hand over Leslie's mouth. Blue eyes regarded in him mock hurt.

"Enough." Eddie said firmly. Gideon didn't need to know how much Eddie had moped because of their little argument earlier on the relationship. "Now if you've finished scoping out my boyfriend, we have more important things to attend to. Like a possessed friend." Leslie's eyes widened and Eddie could have kicked himself.

Boyfriend? Shit, he hadn't meant that to come out. What the hell would Gideon think about that?

He tried to cast an inconspicuous look at Gideon to see what the reaction was to that word. Strangely enough, Gideon didn't look all that fazed, but looked rather thoughtfully at Eddie.

He swallowed. "Come on. Let's do this." He and Gideon followed Leslie into the house. The expression on Gideon's face as he took in Leslie's choice of attire was precious. Eddie sniggered. He guessed Gideon wasn't used to seeing someone sashaying— because Leslie sashayed, he never walked—in tight black trousers that left nothing to the imagination, an oversized pink tee shirt sparkled with sequins and a pair of blue Papa Smurf slippers. They were Leslie's "comfort" clothes.

The lounge was dimly lit, and he saw the figure of Taylor lying on the couch. He was muttering softly to himself.

"He paced for hours. I managed to get him into the lounge and he sat down eventually." Leslie said quietly as he sunk deftly to the floor like a long-legged, graceful giraffe. "I tried to get some chamomile tea down him but he wouldn't drink it. Before, he was pacing around the place like a wild man. He was going on about gingerbread again, and kept saying your name. So I called you." He shrugged and glanced over at Gideon. "Sorry to disturb the whole love nest thing you two have going on but I really needed your help." His tone was wry but Eddie heard the worry in it.

He reached over and hugged his friend. "No love nest comes between you, me and a friend in need," he said. He frowned. "What the heck is that on the floor?"

There was a large circle of fine white crystals in the middle of the living room. Leslie looked a little guilty. "It's a ring of salt. You know, when you watch *Buffy*, they always protect themselves from demons and stuff by staying in the salt. I was sitting in the circle until you got here."

His tone was defiant and Eddie wanted to giggle loudly at the thought of Leslie in his Smurf slippers sitting inside a ring of salt. From the look on Gideon's face, the man was having difficulty controlling his laughter too.

Eddie nodded solemnly. "That was quick thinking, Batman. Always a good idea to protect oneself by salt."

Leslie gave him a quick smile as if to say, "Thanks, I knew you'd get it," then turned to look at Taylor. "Tay? Eddie's here, sweetie. Can you maybe wake up and tell him what the problem is?"

Eddie shivered at the blank look in Taylor's eyes as he stared at the far wall. His face was slack, his dark eyes expressionless. His lips moved and Eddie could hear him saying, "The gingerbread house. He's there. He's in trouble. The trees are staring at him and he's so scared. So scared...."

Gideon frowned and knelt down beside him. "Eddie, maybe if you talk to him he might recognise your voice and come out of it. Keep talking to him and maybe you can get through."

Eddie nodded. He cleared his throat and reached over to squeeze Taylor's shoulder. His friend's body was rigid like marble and he was cold. Eddie shivered. "Tay, it's Eddie. Leslie said you've been calling me? Well, I'm here now. What do you want to tell me?"

For a minute, Eddie thought he'd get no response. Then slowly, like a puppet being controlled by invisible strings, Taylor turned his head to stare at Eddie with those unseeing eyes. The sight was chilling and Eddie gasped then felt Gideon's warm hand on his back.

"Keep talking," he whispered as he rubbed circles on Eddie's skin. "You're getting a reaction. I know it's damn spooky but I think he heard you."

Leslie's eyes were focused on the two of them, his gaze soft and longing. He watched the slow circles Gideon was making with eyes that seemed to envy them.

Eddie tried again. "Taylor, talk to me, mate. I know something's up, so tell me what it is. I can't help you if I don't know what the problem is."

Taylor's eyes darkened and Eddie thanked God at least something had provoked a response. Taylor's voice was anguished when he spoke again.

"He's so cold, Eddie. He's in the gingerbread house, and the trees scare him. They shiver and shake and bend over. He doesn't know what else to do, he needs to do this. He's so alone, God, he's so alone…"

Eddie felt the first stirrings of recognition in Taylor's words. There was something about the trees and the gingerbread house that conjured up an old memory, one he thought was from his childhood. But he just couldn't quite get it.

Frustrated, he reached out and clasped Taylor's face between his now chilled hands, trying to ground him, make him explain. As he did so, a sudden dark feeling swept through him. He cried out loudly as the sensation burrowed into his being and flushed his body and mind with pain, guilt, sorrow and anger and fear. It overwhelmed him, swooped in like an eagle plucking its prey from the depths of a cold sea, leaving him trembling.

He vaguely heard Gideon's exclamation of panic and Leslie's frantic entreaties to "come back, Eddie, you arsehole." An image of an old shed and the forbidding vision of tall, dark trees speared his consciousness like an old movie scene, gaunt in its appearance. It was only a brief flash, but with a sudden burst of clarity, Eddie remembered.

He reeled back from Taylor, into Gideon's warm and strong arms as his lover pulled him to his chest, the fear in his eyes evident. Eddie gasped and buried his face into Gideon's chest as he took a heaving breath.

"Jesus, what the hell happened? You just went blank and scared the shit out of me!" Gideon's voice trembled with fear and apprehension. Eddie nodded against his man's beating heart.

"I know the place Taylor is talking about. I saw it. It's an old shed back home, a few miles from my house, set deep in the woods. Luke and I used to play there when we were kids. He always called it the gingerbread house, after Hansel and Gretel, and we used to pretend the witch lived there and was going to eat us." He took another deep breath. "Something's wrong with Luke. I can feel it. That's what Taylor's being trying to tell me. Luke is in trouble." He scrambled to his feet. "I have to call him, find out if he's okay. We'll take it from there."

Eddie pulled out his phone and started scrolling through his contacts.

*****

Gideon took a deep breath. When Eddie had gone all pale and quiet and looked zoned out, Gideon's heart had clenched and he'd gone cold. He didn't really believe in all this clap trap of Taylor being able to have visions but Eddie did and that was what mattered. And that "boyfriend" comment—he hated to admit it but he'd gone all warm and fuzzy inside thinking that was how Eddie thought of him. Gideon rather liked the idea. He'd had the man in his bed for the past few weeks and was definitely taken with him. He thought he might even want to keep him, and wasn't that a turn up for the books? Eddie was a definite nightmare deterrent, something Gideon was ever thankful for. He'd known peace for the first time in a long time.

Taylor was now lying quiet on the couch, his face softened and his body more relaxed. It was as if he knew his job was done. Leslie bent down and smoothed dark curls off his forehead as he murmured sweet nothings to his friend, all the time casting anxious glances at Eddie and Gideon. Eddie sat at the dining table, on his phone, looking pale but decidedly better than when he'd all gone spaced out.

"Luke's not answering; it's just going to voice mail. I need to call his mum." He dialled another number, his face anxious. His face lit up as someone obviously answered their phone.

"Aunt Claire? It's Eddie. Yes I know what time it is but this couldn't wait. I'm so sorry to wake you up. "

There was a squawking noise from the other side and Gideon grimaced. They didn't sound very happy being woken up at four in the morning. He moved over to stand beside Eddie, placing a hand on his shoulder.

"No, this isn't another drunk prank call. And I only did that a couple of times." Eddie's voice was aggrieved. Gideon grinned despite the situation at the thought of his man placing rambling drunken calls to his family. "Can you please do me a favour? Can you tell me if Luke's home? He's not answering his phone."

More squawking and Eddie's face brightened. "Oh, he is? Are you sure?" He hesitated. "Can you do me a really big favour? Can you check his place, make sure he's there for me? I've just had this bad feeling about him…" His voice trailed off and he rolled his eyes, looking as cute as hell to Gideon. Leslie was watching them both as if he were at a tennis match, his eyes flitting from Gideon to Eddie and back. Taylor was quiet now, seemingly sleeping and Gideon envied him.

Eddie's voice got louder. "Please, Aunt Claire. He's just in the guest cottage, please can you wander down and check and see he's okay?" He huffed and scowled at his phone as he mouthed, "She can be such a pain in the arse. I don't know how poor Luke puts up with her."

"She's his mum," Gideon said with a grin. "You put up with a lot when it's your mother."

Eddie frowned. "Well, she finally said she'd check. Luke lives in the little guest annexe just off the house. He came home at ten p.m. apparently. She saw his car pull in." He waited, tapping his other hand impatiently on the wooden table. The constant noise was driving Gideon crazy. He reached out and stroked Eddie's cheek tenderly.

"Stop that. I hate repetitive sounds like that. It makes me want to scream."

Eddie smiled wanly. "Sorry. It's just something I do when I'm nervous or worried." He leaned forward and planted a soft kiss on Gideon's cheek.

Leslie let out a deep sigh. "Oh my God, you two are so damn cute together. Just fucking adorable." His voice sounded like he'd just seen Cinderella with her prince. "I hope one day I'll find someone like you have, Eddie. Nobody seems to want me." His voice was sad.

Gideon wasn't sure what to say. "I'm sure one day you'll find that special someone."

Leslie gazed at him with sad, puppy-dog eyes.

Gideon coughed uncomfortably, feeling he needed to say more to this pixie-like young man with eyes like skies of cerulean blue. "I mean, you're a nice-looking guy and very sweet, any man would be glad to have you at his side."

Eddie flashed a beaming, approving smile at him, one that turned Gideon's insides to jelly and gave him an instant boner. The man had that effect on him when he so clearly showed his feelings. It was something Gideon wasn't used to doing but was getting easier with Eddie in his life.

Leslie certainly looked happier with his words. "Ooh, Eddie, you need to keep this one. He's adorable." He looked hopeful. "Do you have a brother and does he swing my way?"

Gideon stared at him. "Err, no, I don't have a brother."

Leslie sighed. "Pity." He looked at Eddie. "Jesus, how far is your cousin's flat? Barbados? Haven't they checked he's there yet?"

Eddie frowned. "There's a lot of noise and I can hear Aunt Claire saying something. And I think that's my Uncle Dave in the background. Hello? Hello?" He shouted into the phone and waited impatiently. He made to start tapping his fingers again but a glare from Gideon stayed his fingers.

Eddie's face whitened. "Aunt Claire. He's not there? You found what? Oh God, please don't say that." His voice tailed to a whisper and the stunned look on his face and tightening of his shoulders made Gideon apprehensive.

Eddie looked up at Gideon. "He's not there. They found a note in his room, a suicide note. Oh God, Luke, what the hell have you done?"

Gideon reached over and took the phone from Eddie's trembling fingers. He spoke into it as he placed a warm and comforting hand on his boyfriend's back.

"This is Gideon, I'm a friend of Eddie's." He didn't want to mistakenly out Eddie to his other family members by saying he was the boyfriend, although from what he knew of Eddie it wasn't something he hid. "What does the note say?"

Eddie's aunt's voice trembled as she replied. "He says he's sorry but he can't bear the guilt anymore and he's very confused about things. He wants us not to worry, says he's going somewhere better." Her voice finally cracked. "Oh my God, where is my boy?"

Gideon closed his eyes at the anguish in that tone. "Ma'am, I'm going to put Eddie back on the phone. He thinks he knows where your son might be." He handed the phone to Eddie who nodded.

"That's what Taylor's been trying to tell me. The old shed."

Gideon nodded. "I might not believe in this stuff, but we have no other options at the moment. Tell your aunt to go to that old place, and check it out. It's worth the shot isn't it?"

Eddie nodded in stunned silence then lifted the phone to his ear. "Aunt Claire? Listen to me. You and Uncle Dave need to go the old Watson place in the woods down the road. The old shed there where Luke and I used to play. I think he might be there."

His voice rose slightly. "I just have a feeling, that's all. If he's not home, then he has to be somewhere else and he hasn't taken his car, you said. Please, just get Uncle Dave to shoot out there now. We've got nothing to lose—except Luke."

Those final words seemed to end the debate and Eddie closed in his eyes in a gesture of relief. His body relaxed and Gideon felt a swell of tenderness that his normally confident chef looked so vulnerable.

"Good, tell him to make it quick. And phone me the minute you hear anything. As soon as I hear from you, I'll be travelling up there to see what the hell Luke is playing at." His lips set in a mutinous line, one Gideon recognised well. "The boss owes me some time off so I'm sure he'll agree to me taking it." His eyes sought Gideon's, defiant.

Gideon chuckled softly at Eddie's fierceness, despite the circumstances. "Take all the time you need. I'm going with you anyway."

Eddie's face lit up and a smile split his face. Gideon loved the fact he could please him just by something simple like being there for him.

"You are? That's great, thanks."

Leslie sighed, a deep, heartfelt one that echoed in the room. "Just beautiful," he murmured to himself as he stroked Taylor's sleeping cheek.

Gideon swore the man had tears in his eyes. Uncomfortable, he wandered to the window to gaze into the darkness beyond. Eddie paced around the room, muttering, and Gideon finally lost patience with his agitation and scowled as he moved toward him. Eddie looked up in surprise as he was pulled into a bear hug.

"For God's sake," Gideon grumbled. "Stop bouncing up and down like a cat in a cage. It's driving me crazy." His hands stroked down Eddie's spine and Eddie shivered. He melted against his body, his mouth seeking Gideon's throat as he trailed soft kisses along his skin.

"I thought you liked it when I bounced up and down," he said wickedly and Gideon's face flushed as Leslie gave a cackle.

"Oh touché, Eddie. Great comeback on that one." Leslie's eyes gleamed. "The thought of you two doing it like that makes me really hot." His face became hopeful. "Maybe one day I can be a voyeur?" He giggled at the glares he got from both Gideon and Eddie in return. "Or maybe not..." His voice trailed off and he turned his attention once again to the dozing Taylor.

Eddie was still jittery and Gideon led him to the couch and made him sit down, seating himself beside him. "You need to be patient," he said softly. "I know it's scary but we need to have faith that they'll find Luke and he'll be okay."

Eddie nodded, his face pale. "I don't know what would drive him to try and kill himself," he said, his voice trembling. "I mean, I should have been there for him; I knew he wanted to talk to me."

"Don't go blaming yourself," Gideon said gruffly. "You're not responsible for your cousin's actions. All you can do is be there for him when they find him." Privately he felt a little unsure about a positive outcome but he needed to keep Eddie's spirits up.

Eddie sighed, his eyes closing. He looked exhausted. "I hope they call back soon." Gideon held him and felt Eddie's body slowly relax as he fell into sleep. He looked over at Leslie, who was watching them.

"How's Taylor?" he asked quietly, not wanting to wake Eddie. "Is he okay, do you think?"

Leslie leaned back and stretched. "He seems fine. Sleeping at least, just like your man." His mouth split in a huge yawn. "I'm knackered myself but there's no way I'll fall asleep." He gestured at Eddie. "You really like my mate, huh? Eddie's good people. You'd better treat him right or you'll feel the sharp end of my longest and thinnest stiletto heels in your balls."

Said balls scrunched up at that threat. "I've no intention of treating Ed badly," Gideon said with a scowl. "He's a grown man. He can take care of himself without some heel-wearing diva doing it for him."

Leslie flapped a hand airily. "Oh make no mistake about this diva, girlfriend. I've been known to hurt the balls of bigger men than you, Gideon Trent, and you really should heed my warning." His dark eyes flashed and Gideon felt a slight sense of unease.

This slight, effeminate man was a little more than he looked if that glint in his eye was anything to go by.

Leslie smirked. "You do know he hates being called Ed?" he murmured. "He says it makes him sound like a donkey."

Gideon blinked. "A donkey?" he said faintly.

Leslie's long lashes fluttered in amusement around darkened, sleep-deprived eyes. "The donkey from the TV series *Mister Ed*?" He shook his head soulfully at what must have been Gideon's blank and mystified look. "Oh Giddy, you have led a sheltered life. I feel sorry for your arse not having the delight that is *Mister Ed*." His smile grew wider. "I'll have to tell Eddie to educate you somewhat."

Gideon glared at him. His own eyes were gritty and sore from the lack of sleep and Leslie was seriously not helping. "First, don't call me bloody Giddy. I hate it. Secondly, Mister Ed was actually a horse. And you can keep that show to yourself, thanks very much." He grimaced. "It's bad enough I have to sit and watch *Flog It!* with Eddie because he has this unholy fascination with all things antique and he gets off watching other people selling their crap."

Leslie's eyes widened. "Really? He was a horse? I could have sworn he was an ass." He giggled then grinned. "Wow, you can be quite grouchy, can't you? I don't think Eddie relieves your tension enough." He winked. "Dr. Leslie proposes a lot more blow jobs for you to get rid of that sexual frustration you have."

Gideon opened his mouth to retort that he was getting blown quite regularly fuck you very much but spotted the wicked glint in Leslie's eyes and stopped. "Well, at least *I'm* getting some," he finally said loftily.

Leslie cackled and waved long fingers in his direction. "Get you, all snarky and quick-witted."

In spite of Leslie's comment, Gideon saw the sudden flash of pain in his eyes which made Gideon feel like a heel. He pressed his lips together lest he put his foot in it again. Eddie had told him all about Leslie's abortive relationships and how his friend thought he'd never find Mr. Right.

"I'm sorry. I shouldn't have said that," he muttered. "Blame the fact it's the middle of the bloody morning and I need more sleep. I can be a bastard when I'm tired."

Leslie shrugged. "No worries." He reached out and brushed his hand against the sleeping Taylor's cheek. "When you're right, you're right." He glanced over at Gideon, who shifted uncomfortably. "I wish I had something like what you and Eddie have. It looks pretty special to me."

Gideon looked over at the slumbering Eddie. "I'm not sure about special, but I like the guy."

Leslie cocked his head like a curious parrot. "You do, don't you? I can see it on your face when you look at him. My Eddie has gone and got himself a big, bad protector." Despite the apparent snarkiness of the words, Gideon heard the approval in Leslie's voice. He felt a little uneasy about Leslie's words. Since when he had stooped to wearing his emotions on his face?

It was all a bit confusing. To the point where, when he heard Eddie's voice and saw his face, his heart leapt in his chest like a salmon in mid-stream. Waking up to warm man in his bed, seeing Eddie's softly snoring face only inches from his…

Knowing he's all mine.

His stomach clenched.

Fuck. He was in so deep in such a short time; it was like something out of a penny dreadful.

"You know, I can hear the wheel spinning from here." Leslie's amused voice cut into Gideon's panicked thoughts like a tinkling bell. "That hamster seems to be peddling mighty fast."

Gideon stared frostily at Leslie. "What the hell are you talking about?"

Leslie chuckled. "Taylor might be the real psychic here but I have a few talents of my own." He frowned, his mouth pursing into an adorable pout.

Even Gideon appreciated a twinky pout.

"You were standing there wondering what the hell was happening and how you got so invested in Eddie so fast. It was written all over your face." His own face softened. "I'm glad for both of you, so don't fight it, Gideon. Eddie thinks the world of you."

A sleepy voice interrupted. "Eddie is now awake and wondering what the hell the two of you are talking about."

Gideon turned to see Eddie's still-unfocused eyes staring at him with some trepidation. "Leslie, what the heck have you been saying to Gideon? He looks like the axe is about to fall. The whole deer-in-the-headlights thing."

"Oh, nothing. We were just passing the time." Leslie looked at the clock on the wall and frowned. "Talking of which, when the fuck are your auntie and uncle going to call back? They should have found your cousin by now surely."

Eddie's face darkened. "Unless there's a problem and they had to call the police, or an ambulance," he said softly, the fear in his eyes causing Gideon's chest to tighten. He walked over to his boyfriend and sat down beside him, drawing him into his arms.

"Don't assume the worst," he murmured. "If they haven't called in another fifteen minutes, we'll call them back for an update."

Eddie reached up and captured Gideon's mouth in a tender kiss that made him wish they were alone so he could visit more upon Eddie's person than just his lips. Eddie's breath was warm, slightly stale with the faint taste of mint. When he finally released Gideon's mouth, Gideon gazed into green eyes that promised so much.

"Thanks for doing this with me," Eddie whispered. He gently brushed a strand of hair from Gideon's cheek and looked over Leslie who was misty eyed.

Eddie grinned. "Please don't start bawling, Leslie. I think Gideon might run for the hills if you did."

As Leslie sniffed and blinked back obvious tears, Eddie's phone rang. Eddie's face whitened and he looked at the innocent item lying on the side table as if it might grow teeth and rip him to shreds. He reached out with trembling hands and picked it up, as Gideon laid a comforting hand against his back.

"Hello? Aunt Claire?" A squawk on the other end of the phone answered his enquiry.

Taylor started suddenly and sat up with an exhale of air and a look of panic in his eyes. "What's going on, guys?" His voice was throaty, almost raw, and he grimaced and cleared his throat. "Is everything okay?"

Leslie reached out a hand and patted Taylor's shoulder. "It's all under control, Tay. You had one of your turns then fell asleep. Now we're about to find out what's going on." His voice shook a little but he smiled at Taylor who still looked bemused. "Eddie's just on the phone to his family to check on his cousin, Luke, who decided he'd had enough of life." He smiled softly at the panicked expression on Taylor's face. "Don't worry. We're on the case."

Eddie's face was tight as he listened to the conversation taking place and Gideon continued reassuring him with slight strokes to his back. Finally Eddie's shoulders relaxed and he closed his eyes as a look of relief crossed his face.

"Luke's all right," he said, his voice trembling. "He took pills but they managed to get to him in time. He's on his way to the hospital now." Anxious eyes gazed over at Gideon. "Can we go see him, Gideon? Will you drive me up there?" At Gideon's firm nod, Eddie's face softened and he spoke back into his mobile. "Yes, I'm on my way up to see the stupid bastard. I'll find out what's going on, Aunt Claire, I promise. Even if I have to string him up by the balls and torture it out of him." His face was fierce and Gideon's heart stuttered with affection at the look of determination on his man's face.

"We'll go up there in a few hours once we've both gotten some sleep," he said quietly. He forestalled Eddie's protest. "We're both knackered, Eddie. There's no point me driving when I'm tired. We want to get there in one piece."

Eddie's face was mutinous. "But I want to see Luke," he muttered as he passed a hand over tired, swollen eyes. Gideon hid a smile. His lover sounded like a sulky child. He nodded. "And we will. But first we're going to catch some shut-eye. Where's your room?"

He raised an enquiring eyebrow.

Eddie scowled. "Fine. Have it your way. Browbeat the exhausted, traumatised person into submission. Let him worry about his favourite cousin languishing in a hospital room with no one to wake up to." He waited, no doubt hoping Gideon would feel guilty and have a change of heart. Gideon continued gazing at him patiently.

Taylor snorted tiredly. "Looks like you've met your match, Eddie, my friend. I like this one. He doesn't take your crap." He stood up and stretched as Eddie regarded him with narrowed eyes.

"You're supposed to be on my side."

Taylor shrugged. "I agree with Gideon. At least I think this is Gideon. We haven't been formally introduced." He grinned tiredly and Gideon nodded. "Pleased to meet you. Now, Edster, have you seen yourself? You look like crap. I'm glad your cousin is okay. Maybe you should take your man off to bed and go and get some sleep. I'm going to do the same." He reached out and touched Leslie's cheek tenderly. "You've been so busy taking care of me and no one's been looking after you. So if you want to come and sleep with me and cuddle, I'm game. You can tell me what I've been up to." He yawned and smiled at them all. "Goodnight you lot. Eddie, if I don't see you before you leave, stay safe and call me when you get to Norfolk. Let me know how Luke's doing." He nodded at Gideon. "Take care of my friend, please. You're good for him. And he's definitely good for you. Maybe he can chase those nightmares away for good." He winked. "And I have a feeling you'll be cooking again in no time."

Gideon's jaw dropped. How the hell did he know about all this? He supposed Eddie had told him. And that comment about cooking? Was he talking metaphorically—in the bedroom cooking, or something else?

Taylor turned and left. Leslie watched him fondly then turned to Eddie and Gideon.

"A man doesn't get an offer to cuddle often so I'm going to take advantage of it." He reached over and gave Eddie a huge hug. Then he turned to Gideon and reached out his arms. Gideon scowled. "I'm not the hugging type—umff." His words were cut off as Leslie enveloped him in a clutch than nearly cut off his air supply. It was like being tackled by an octopus. A very nice, firm-bodied and warm octopus. Gideon felt guilty at even thinking the thought. Resigned to his fate, he let Leslie finish his embrace and step back. The younger man's eyes were shiny.

"You two take care of each other, and Eddie, call me too when you get to Norfolk. G'night." He disappeared into the hallway. Gideon looked at Eddie.

"Are he and Taylor, uhm, you know? Doing the dirty together?"

Eddie chuckled tiredly. "Not that I know of. They have this rather strange relationship and often sleep in each other's beds but I don't think they've fucked each other. Taylor's a bit of a player although he's never brought anyone home here. And I was too busy mooning over you to give a damn what they were up to."

Gideon felt warmth flush his body and he reached out his arms. Eddie came into them willingly. He turned his face up for a kiss and Gideon obliged. Warm male in his arms, soft lips on his with a hint of stubble, a tongue that delved into the far reaches of his mouth and made him breathless. Gideon knew, not for the first time, he was a goner, well and truly fallen. His body responded to Eddie's passionate kiss and he pressed his hips against his boyfriend's, needing him, wanting him but not sure if Eddie was in the mood. When Eddie's hands found his jeans zipper and pulled it down to reach inside and stroke Gideon's upright and straining cock, he had his answer.

"Don't start something you don't intend to finish," Gideon growled in pleasure at Eddie's firm, hot strokes on his prick, and his hips pushed toward Eddie's in anticipation. Eddie's eyes opened in mock surprise, their green depths drawing Gideon in.

"Them's fighting words." His fingers grew stronger and Gideon hitched a breath as the sensations overwhelmed him. "I thought you deserved a little reward for being so nice to me and agreeing to take me home. But I can always leave it for another day...."

His hand left Gideon's cock and Gideon snarled. "Don't you fucking dare."

He gasped in relief as Eddie's hand resumed its teasing on his prick and his warm breath huffed against Gideon's throat. Eddie's mouth made warm trails down Gideon's overheated skin, tongue flicking at the sweat, drinking him in, and Gideon gasped. "Christ, just keep that up. I'm not going to last long. What the hell do you do to me anyway? I'm like a horny teenager when you're around."

Eddie nipped on Gideon's shoulder, biting through the fabric and making Gideon hiss in both pain and pleasure. "I just want you," he murmured. "A lot. Can't you feel?" He took Gideon's hand with his free hand and dragged it down to his crotch. "You have a choice. You can either jack me off now with you or you can give me a blow job when we go to bed. Which one is it going to be?"

He didn't wait for a reply. The fingers on Gideon's cock gave one final tug and Eddie whispered into his ear, "Come for me. I want to see you let loose."

Gideon's breath left him at those erotically charged words and his balls crept up into his groin. He grunted and groaned with the force of his orgasm. It shot through his cock, covering Eddie's hand with stickiness and leaving Gideon boneless. "Good Christ, Eddie," he rasped. "Are you trying to bloody kill me?"

Eddie chuckled. "I guess it's going to be a BJ then." He removed his hand from Gideon's sticky cock and wiped it on his jeans. Gideon collapsed against the wall, his now spent prick peeking out of his jeans. Eddie tut-tutted and tucked him away, pulling the zip up and giving him a cheeky grin. He unzipped his own chinos and softly palmed what looked to Gideon like a very impressive erection.

"Come on, big guy. Little Eddie's waiting for you to wrap those sexy lips around him and blow him to kingdom come. That'll make me sleep and then we'll be ready for the drive home."

He disappeared into the hallway leaving Gideon still a little unsteady. Their sex life was very good, incredible, in fact, but when Eddie took charge like that, and whispered dirty things into his ear, it turned Gideon on no end. Eddie had a definite dominant streak and Gideon? Well, Gideon was quite happy to play along, something he thought he'd never do with another man.

As he walked the dark hallway toward Eddie's room, a rush of delight assailing him at the thought he'd soon have Eddie's lovely cock in his mouth, giving him pleasure and making him come so he could swallow every last drop, Gideon wondered not for the first time how this would all end. He knew he wanted Eddie around for a long time to come but he had no idea whether Eddie felt the same way. As he entered the bedroom and saw Eddie lying on the bed stark naked, his glistening cock already in hand as he stroked himself, Gideon told himself those thoughts could wait. Right now, he had something better to do.

Chapter 15

The drive late the following morning to Eddie's hometown of Diss was without incident and they made it in good time. There had been a few stops along the way for the usual coffee breaks but by the time midday rolled around, Eddie and Gideon were walking into the hospital. Eddie managed to catch a glimpse of his sleeping cousin and placed a soft kiss on his forehead with the whispered promise to come back later. Luke's stomach had been pumped and the nurse—a large, stern-looking woman Eddie found rather scary—had told them he was doing well but would probably be away with the fairies for a while.

It didn't take long for them to track down Eddie's aunt and uncle. They were sitting in the cafeteria looking tired and drained. Claire rushed over to her nephew, enveloping him in a fierce hug. She threw a questioning glance at Gideon. Claire was a tiny woman, five-foot-and-a-bit with a petite frame and dark blonde hair streaked with grey. Her husband Dave, though, was a mountain; he'd played rugby in his earlier years and it showed in his stock frame and muscled legs and arms. His bald head shone in the glare of the harsh hospital lighting.

Eddie turned to introduce Gideon to his aunt and uncle. "This is my boyfriend, Gideon. He owns the restaurant I chef in. Gideon, Aunt Claire and Uncle Dave."

Hands were shaken, appraisals made, Dave's keen blue eyes assessing Gideon and obviously approving as he gave a little nod to Eddie. There was the faint trace of an approving grin on his face despite the circumstances. Soon they were seated at the cafeteria table over steaming cups of tasteless coffee in plastic cups.

"So what happened?" Eddie was itching to find out what had driven Luke to try and kill himself. "I know he was bit off lately but I thought maybe he'd had a row with Rachel and needed a referee."

Claire glanced at her husband then at Eddie. "He broke up with Rachel two months ago." Eddie's eyes widened. "I had no idea! The couple of times I spoke to him, he never mentioned it. God, what happened?"

Dave gave a great sigh. "We don't know. Luke simply said it was over and wouldn't tell us why. I spoke to Rachel's parents and all they told me was that Luke had decided it wasn't working and he needed to be on his own. Rachel was upset but they'd only been going out four months so I expect she'll get over it soon enough. She's young and sweet."

Eddie was flabbergasted. Luke wasn't the sort to cut and run. Something momentous must have happened to make him hurt Rachel like that. Eddie had thought they were really good together.

I just have to talk to him.

He stood up. "I'm going to go and see whether he's awake," he said. "If not I'll bloody pinch the shit out of him secretly so that scary nurse doesn't see me. He really needs to tell us what the hell is going on in that damned head of his."

"Do you want me to come with you?" Gideon asked softly. Eddie shook his head.

"I'll be fine, thanks. He may tell me more if it's just me. Of course, you might want to speak to him first," he looked at Claire and Dave, "so shall I let you do that before I get hold of him?"

Dave shook his head. "If anyone can get into his head and find out what's been going on, it's you, Edster. You and Luke have been as close as brothers in the past and he'll talk to you. God knows we tried to. You go ahead. We'll stop by in a little while."

Eddie nodded and turned to his boyfriend. "Okay. I'll see you later, baby." He leaned down and kissed Gideon on the lips then turned and walked down the corridor. A few minutes later he was sitting by his cousin's bedside, debating which part of him to pinch into wakefulness, when Luke stirred and his eyes opened. They were unfocused and drowsy but lit up when he saw Eddie sitting at his bedside.

"Eddie." His voice was husky, no doubt from the tube that had been forced down his throat to pump out his stomach contents. "I knew you'd come."

Eddie leaned over and clasped Luke's cold hand. "You know it, cuz. I just wish you'd waited for me before doing something stupid. I'm really glad you're all right. Everyone was worried about you."

Luke's eyes filled with tears. "I'm so sorry, Eddie. I really fucked up, didn't I. Mum and Dad must be so damn mad with me." He sniffled and tears ran down his pale cheeks as he struggled up in bed. Eddie stood up and gently pushed him down back against the pillows.

"Don't be so bloody daft. Your mum and dad are just pleased you're safe. A little bewildered as to why you'd want to do such a damn foolish thing, as we all are, but just happy you're still with us."

Eddie sat back down, gently stroking Luke's hand and waiting until the younger man had recovered before pressing on. His stomach churned with guilt and he had something he needed to say before it ripped him apart. The words came out like a flood. "I knew you were upset about something, but I never thought you'd take something this far. I thought it was maybe a problem with Rachel; that you'd had an argument, but nothing serious enough to try and kill yourself. If I'd known how desperate you were, I'd have been here sooner, honest, Luke. You have to believe me. I was so damn busy with my own life I wasn't there for you. But I'm here now and I want to help, Luke."

Luke's eyes had widened at Eddie's verbal diarrhoea and his red-rimmed blue eyes looked panicked. He opened his mouth to say something and Eddie rushed ahead.

"I promise I'll stick around until you feel better and we can deal with whatever is on your mind—"

There was a slight snort from the doorway and Eddie turned to see Gideon standing there, arms crossed against his chest as he leaned against the door frame. Even in Eddie's state he could still appreciate the broad chest and sexy grin of his lover.

Gideon moved into the room. "Eddie, sweetheart, you've terrified your poor cousin from the looks of it. The man can't get a word in edgeways with you spouting off like a water fountain." He leaned down and kissed Eddie's lips which were beginning to pout at Gideon's words.

The kiss was warm and gentle and Eddie closed his eyes in pleasure. He knew he'd said he could do this on his own but he was really glad Gideon was with him. When the pressure of Gideon's mouth disappeared, Eddie opened his eyes. He found Gideon arranging his tall frame in a small visitor's chair.

"I wanted to be here with you," he murmured quietly. "Just pretend I'm not here."

Luke's eyes were completely focused on him and Eddie, an expression of both yearning and despair etched across his elfin face.

"Wow, Eddie. You have a real boyfriend." His whispered words made Eddie fidget.

"Oi, you. What do you mean a *real boyfriend*?" His tone was teasing. He knew his track record hadn't been all that good in the past. He'd not really counted Seb, the lanky skater boy, Daniel the two-timing bitch and Jasper, the crazy vegetarian as real boyfriends. Fuck buddies to start, with the hope that things might develop into a lasting relationship, but none of them had made it further.

Gideon smirked at him.

Eddie scowled and sat down on the bed next to Luke. "And stop distracting me. You and me, we have some talking to do. Maybe not right now but when you're feeling better."

He was being a lot more patient than he felt, as he was desperate to find out what had prompted Luke's actions.

Luke swallowed and leaned back against the pillows, closing his eyes "I just lost it, Edster. I had a really shitty couple of weeks and I did something I'm not proud of and…" His voice tailed off. "It all got too much."

Eddie reached over and caressed his cousin's cheek. "Nothing you could have done or found out would have been enough to do what you did. I know you're a good person—"

"I'm a fucking shitty person!" Luke's voice grew stronger and the look of disgust on his face threw Eddie. Luke's eyes were dark, his mouth twisted into an ugly grimace. "I made someone hurt themselves because I was a bastard, a fucking coward. If I'd had more damn guts Francis wouldn't be lying in a hospital with his wrists slashed. I deserve to be here."

His voice cracked and his slight frame shook with sobs as he cried, tears of anguish coursing down his cheeks. Eddie stared at him in stupefaction. Gideon leaned forward and spoke quietly, his voice steady, calming.

"Luke, you're seventeen years old. We do stupid things at that age." He gave a dry laugh. "Hell, we do stupid things at my age. Ask Eddie. He'll tell you I can be a complete arsehole myself." His soft, self-deprecating grin at Eddie seemed to soothe Luke, who took a shuddering breath. "But whatever you did, you can fix it, make it right. You don't deserve to die for being stupid." He reached out and took Luke's hand in his. Eddie swallowed, his throat constricting at the tenderness on Gideon's face for someone he didn't even know.

"You need to talk to your cousin, tell him what happened. Eddie's a good listener. If you want me to leave, I will." He stood up to go but Luke pulled him back down.

"No, stay. I don't mind you being here." He looked down at the white sheet, his hands plucking invisible threads as his chest heaved with emotion. When he looked up at Eddie, his face was bleak.

"Eddie, you knew you were gay when you were really young, didn't you? I remember you telling me about the time you saw Dennis Manning naked in the locker room after a rugby game when you were only thirteen. You said you got such a boner at his naked arse and the look of his package that you had to jack off in the bathroom." Luke smiled faintly and Eddie now knew where this was going. His face flushed as Gideon looked over at him, and Eddie could see he was trying to withhold his laughter.

Eddie shifted uncomfortably. "I don't think I *quite* put it that way, Luke," he began, knowing that was exactly how he'd put it. The sight of the very manly Dennis in all his rosy glory after just coming out the shower had given him an erection that had threatened to poke his teammates' eyes out. Luckily he'd had a pile of dirty towels in his arms at the time and managed to hide his arousal until he could sort it out five minutes later.

Gideon chuckled, a sexy sound that turned Eddie's bones to mush. "I'm having a bit of a problem visualising you playing rugby, Eddie. You're not exactly built for rugger."

Eddie glared at him. "I was only in the team a few weeks. The coach told me I was better suited for other sports like running, as I had some co-ordination problems." He heard the agitation in his voice. "I only smacked into the guys a few time when I was running with the ball. It wasn't my fault they all got in the bloody way."

Gideon's shoulders shook with silent laughter and even Luke had a wide smile on his face. For a moment, it was as if everything was all right with the world and Eddie was happy to be the brunt of the amusement if it made his cousin smile and forget for a while.

Gideon snorted. "Hell, I can just see you, all adorably klutzy on the field. God, you are so damn cute."

"Yeah, well, let's see how cute I can be when you beg me to suck you off," Eddie said acerbically. "Then we'll see how klutzy I can be when I miss your dick with my mouth."

Gideon was giggling now and didn't Eddie think *that* was adorable. His man *didn't* giggle.

Finally both Luke and Gideon stopped sniggering and Eddie sat in mock injury next to his boyfriend who still had a leer on his face. Luke looked slightly better, having more colour in face as he gripped the covers and smoothed his fingers over the fabric.

"We got sidetracked, sorry," Eddie said softly. "I guess we should hear the rest of your story."

Luke nodded. "You can probably guess where it's going," he murmured. His bright blue eyes gazed over at Eddie, weariness in their depths. "I'm bisexual, gay, whatever. I've been…seeing this guy from college. We've got together a few times." He sighed heavily. "I had to break up with Rachel. She didn't take it too well." His face darkened. "Francis and I really clicked together, and she found me kissing him in my room when we were studying. I didn't want to cheat on her, but the sex—what we had was nothing like what Francis and I had. That was explosive." His face coloured pink. "Well, you two know what that's like. It just felt so much better being with a guy."

Eddie nodded. "No argument from me there. So when did you discover this whole 'I like men better' thing?"

"The last year I've just felt…unsettled, not sure why I didn't want to make out with girls as much as I used to. That's why I started going out with Rachel. I thought maybe it would solve my problem." He shrugged. "It didn't. There's this guy, Francis, and he was really sweet, so gentle and clever." He looked stricken. "He was going through a rough time. His mum and dad died a year ago in a car accident and he lives now with his uncle. He was still cut up about it; he was very close to his folks. We used to get together after school, go for coffee, hang out. He was helping me with my trigonometry, because I'm pants at it." His voice choked up. "I didn't want anyone to know about us so we kept it a secret. I wanted to find out if it was the real me before I told my folks or you. Maybe it was just a phase, maybe I just wanted to experiment."

Gideon nodded, his eyes compassionate. "I can understand that. It can a very confusing time, finding out your sexual identity. You needed time to process things, make sure you were comfortable before you told anyone else."

Luke nodded, his eyes dull. "But I fucked it up. I came out into the courtyard at school one day a couple of weeks ago and these guys were harassing Francis. They had his back pack and they were calling him names. Ugly names. Telling him he was a queer boy, that he liked to suck cock. He saw me and his eyes lit up. He thought I was going to help him." His voice broke. "But I didn't. I walked away and let them torment him. I didn't want to out myself. I thought they'd just pick on him then let him go." He heaved a breath and tears welled in his eyes. Eddie moved forward and laid a comforting arm around Luke's shaking shoulders.

Gideon's face was grim. Whether it was at Luke's actions or the homophobic taunts of the other boys, Eddie didn't know. He hoped the latter.

Luke's words came in between halting breaths. "They beat him up when he tried to fight back. He knew he didn't stand a chance again them but still he tried. My Francis, who'd never thrown a punch in his life. He managed to get home and when I tried calling him later to tell him I was sorry, he wouldn't talk to me."

Luke's voice was flat. "I tried for two days to see him, tell him I'd fucked up and I could understand why he hated me. I stopped calling him. He was better off without me anyway." The pain in his voice made Eddie's heart ache. "I took a few days out, disappeared by myself to the old abandoned barge on the river." He looked at Eddie guiltily. "I wasn't with anyone when you called me that day. I'd been drinking and thinking about jumping into the river. Your call made me think twice."

He fiddled with the seam in the blanket. "Then the next thing I knew a few days ago, I heard Francis had been taken to hospital. He tried to slash his wrists. He left a note for his uncle saying he couldn't cope with everything, the bullying, me not being there for him. But he also said he forgave me for walking away, he understood. That was the worst part. I didn't deserve forgiveness." Luke was sobbing again.

Eddie let out a shocked gasp and Gideon's face grew grimmer.

"The doctor said he hadn't cut too deep, that he was lucky. He did it the wrong way."

The dead look on Luke's face hit at Eddie's heart, making his chest tight and leaving his throat dry as tears prickled behind his eyes. He pulled Luke into his arms as the younger man dissolved into heart-wrenching sobs. His eyes met Gideon's across Luke's dark brown head and the look of understanding and love in Gideon's beautiful brown eyes was Eddie's undoing. Emotional as he was holding his weeping cousin, Eddie realised something.

I am so *in love with him. God, what the hell do I do now? What if he doesn't feel the same way? He might look at me that way but it hasn't been that long and this man has dug into my soul and I'm damned if I know what to do about it.*

He tried to forget the turmoil circling like an eagle in his head and concentrate on the man in his arms. "Luke, honey, it's going to be all right. Francis is still alive and so are you. The two of you will get a chance to talk this out, you have to believe that. Maybe I can go and see him, say hello from you. Is he still here in the hospital, or has he been discharged?"

Eddie's shuddering breaths started to abate. "He…he's still here. In a ward above." He grasped at Eddie's shoulder. "You have to go and see him for me. Tell him he deserves better than me, that he can find someone else who will treat him like he deserves. He's really special, Ed. You have to make him see that."

"You can tell me yourself, Luke," a soft voice said from the doorway. "We've both been bloody idiots."

*****

Gideon turned from his soft stroking of Luke's hand and saw an ethereal, blond young man, pale and wan with light black spectacles on his nose. His thin wrists were covered in bandages. Luke made a sound that was part cry, part sob and Eddie stepped back as the youth moved over to Eddie's side and laid long fingers on his arm. Gideon assumed this was Francis from the tender look he gave Luke.

"You stupid sod," the blond whispered. "Why did you have to go and pull a Francis? You always have to one-up me."

Luke's arms reached out as they embraced.

Francis kissed Luke's lips gently. "We're a couple of selfish wankers, aren't we? Causing our families such trouble." The gentle kiss grew into something a little more heated and Eddie moved away to Gideon's side, feeling like a voyeur.

This is my little cousin making out with his boyfriend for God's sake.

Francis turned to look at them both. "Thanks so much for what you did," he whispered, his eyes tearful. "He's alive and so am I and that's all that really matters. Our folks are going to help us get through this." He ran thin fingers through Luke's straggly hair as Luke gazed at him with adoration. "We'll be fine, love."

"Maybe we should leave them alone," Eddie murmured. "I think they need to clear the air."

Gideon nodded, seeing his boyfriend's eyes suspiciously bright and his heartstrings tugged even more at his sensitive lover's emotional capacity to feel.

"Yeah, let's go grab coffee," he whispered back. His lips found Eddie's neck as he pressed butterfly kisses to the skin. "I feel like just being alone with you for a little while, appreciating what I have. You also need to call Taylor and Leslie or they'll be pissed as hell."

Minutes later they were sitting in the hospital garden, the sun shining down on them as they sipped bad coffee from polystyrene cups. Eddie had made his phone calls to the friends waiting for news and promised to be home soon.

Gideon gazed out with unseeing eyes across the neatly kept lawn and the beds of roses that edged the garden. "I can't imagine how two young men must have felt to get to that depth of despair that they think the world will be a better place without them." He shook his head in bemusement. "Those two will need a lot of support to get through this. At least they have each other it would seem."

"Yep." Eddie smiled at him, a soft, knowing smile." You were great with Luke. I saw another side to my man in there."

Gideon cocked an eyebrow. "Oh, so I have another official title besides the boyfriend now? I'm your *man*?"

Eddie nodded vigorously. "Oh yes. You're definitely mine."

Gideon couldn't suppress a shudder that ran from the tips of his toes to the top of his head at those confident, possessive words. He saw the heat in Eddie's eyes and the slow lick of his lips and he wished that they were anywhere other than in a public place. He wanted to get on his knees and give thanks to the sexy human being that was Eddie Tripp. And while he was on his knees…

Eddie chuckled. "God, you've become so damn transparent. I can see the lust in your eyes. This is a hospital for God's sake. Control yourself." His teasing tone lingered seductively. "Although if you wanted to put on a doctor's gown and play probe the patient with your sexy doctor tool, this patient wouldn't object." His wicked grin and dirty words made Gideon's cock take flight and press to get out of his jeans. He moved to try and accommodate his swelling erection.

"You are a damned tease. You wait until I get you home. I'll show you Doctor Gideon."

Eddie laughed. "As if that's a damn threat. You've got me in a state of anticipation now." He palmed his groin suggestively.

Gideon ignored the blatant gesture. If he didn't he'd be coming in his pants. "Talking of home, how long do you want to stay here? I know you'll want to see that Luke is really okay, although from what I saw earlier he's got a fighting chance at getting over this. As will Francis. I guess the news about him being gay still has to be broken to your aunt and uncle though and I'm guessing that you'll want to be there when Luke does that." He'd already spoken to both Sarah and Carmen who were running his restaurant in his absence. He was itching to get back but knew Eddie would stay behind on his own if he did. So he'd resigned himself to a short unplanned holiday in Norfolk so he could be with him. Carmen had gloatingly told him that he was hooked like a carp and Gideon had used a couple of choice words to tell her what he thought of that statement. It hadn't fazed her in the least.

Eddie's face softened. "You see, that's why I lo-like you. You know me so well." His skin grew rosier and his freckles stood out. Gideon heard the hitch in his voice as he corrected himself and decided not to go there yet.

Best leave that for when all this drama is over. We have enough on our plates at the moment without contending with the L word.

It still gave Gideon a warm and fuzzy feeling that Eddie might feel that way about him.

The fact Gideon still had some issues of his own to resolve didn't escape him. He wasn't wearing rose-tinted glasses but he'd definitely come a long way since meeting Eddie. If two young men could cheat death and still end up together, he was damn sure he could get over his own frailties and make sure it didn't adversely affect their relationship. Nightmares and insecurities about his lost sense be damned; with Eddie's warm body wrapped around him keeping him grounded, Gideon thought the nightmares deserved a rallying "fuck you" to their face. The therapy wasn't doing a bad job of helping either, even though he's begrudged the time and effort. As for the lost of smell and taste, he'd realised seeing Luke and Francis that simply being alive and having someone to care was enough.

. *****

The journey home three days later was one filled with sadness, hope and expectation. Hope that the two young men would find their feet now their parents knew about them. Hope that said parents would support them on their journey to acceptance. Sadness, because Eddie had to leave Luke behind but with the promise of another trip to see them in the near future. Expectation, because both Eddie and Gideon were as horny as goats after not having sex at Eddie's parents' house when Eddie went home to introduce Gideon to them.

The walls of the new-build home that Eddie's family lived in were so thin and Eddie and Gideon so vocal that it simply wasn't worth taking the chance on being heard calling for God in the middle of the night. So there had been the rather abortive attempt at mutual blow jobs in the carport behind Uncle Dave's car while the rest of the family were sleeping late one night. It was far enough from the house for no one to hear the swearing and entreaties to the God of fucking. However, some old dear had been highly vocal in her assertion to her husband that there were effing cats out in the courtyard making an effing noise and Gideon and Eddie had barely contained their sniggers. They had both managed to achieve their objective but it was slightly tarnished by the bucket of water thrown over them in the throes of their passion. They had also managed one fairly successful, highly contorted session in Gideon's car, which had led to Eddie pulling a muscle in his arse and Gideon bruising his hip on the gear stick. All in all, it had been interesting sex but not conducted with quite the finesse they were used to.

Gideon had enjoyed meeting Eddie's folks, Chloe and Frank, and had a great appreciation now for how Eddie had come to be. Frank was warm, rough spoken, with twinkling eyes and he obviously adored his son. Chloe was quirky, rather scary in some ways but one of the most liberal women Gideon had ever met. Even he had blushed when she'd started chatting about gay man sex and the vagaries of rim jobs and blow jobs. Eddie had gone scarlet in embarrassment and gazed at his mother like Chicken Little expecting the sky to fall. It wasn't an experience Gideon wished to experience again anytime soon. While he and Eddie had enjoyed their time there they were both glad to get back on the road home.

They finally got to Gideon's apartment around nine p.m. Eddie's parents had insisted on taking them to a seafood restaurant in the town, one that had a good reputation if Frank was to be believed. Eddie had worked there as a sous-chef in his early start into the food business and the manager still waxed lyrical about his chef talent. It hadn't been a patch on Galileo's in Gideon's opinion but then nothing measured up to his restaurant. It had been a replete but tired couple of men that had finally boarded Ellie for the trip home. They were both glad to walk through the doors into Gideon's flat.

Gideon was in the wet room shower washing off the dirt and grime of the day when he felt a lithe form press itself against his back. The familiar presence of a hard-on indicated it was a man with definite needs and the slow swirl of a warm tongue in his ear made him shiver in delight.

Strong hands ran themselves down his flanks and then reached over to grasp his cock in a firm grip. He smiled and leaned back against Eddie as water ran down their bodies.

"Couldn't wait, sexy?" He teased as his hands reached back and drew Eddie's lips down for a kiss. Eddie's erection slid between his arse cheeks as he pressed himself closer. Gideon's body prickled with need, with want and he turned to face his boyfriend. Eddie's face was pink from the warm water and steam, his freckles standing out starkly against his pale, smooth skin. His deep red hair was plastered to his head like wet, richly coloured silk and some of it fell forward, obscuring eyes that looked at Gideon with such affection and lust.

"I want to be inside you." Eddie's whispered words sent a shiver down Gideon's spine and sent an immediate signal to his already hardened cock to stand up further and take notice. Eddie loved to top him when he was in the mood, and it was an experience and a half. He had a latent instinct to be a bossy and dominating brat when he took control and Gideon loved every minute of that side of his lover. He swiped his tongue lasciviously across Eddie's wet lips and grinned.

"Then do it. You don't need to ask. Take what you want. I'm all yours." The words had never been truer for Gideon. He was definitely no longer a free man, and while his heart wanted to make that very clear to Eddie, his head told him to go slow. He didn't want to ruin this thing they had by jumping the gun.

Eddie growled and bit Gideon's earlobe as his hands reached for the ever-present packet of lube in the shower tray. Gideon heard the rip of the packet and then words from his lips fell like explosive bullets into the steam of the shower. He didn't even know he was going to say them until they were in the air, lingering there like soft droplets of misty liquid.

"Forget the condom. I want this bare."

Eddie stilled behind him and Gideon closed his eyes and swallowed. They'd always used condoms but tonight, he wanted to feel Eddie and *only* him.

"Uhmm, Gideon, that's a new play rule." Eddie sounded unsure although there was a definite hint of excitement in his tone. "I know we're clean because we've talked about it but are you sure?" His hard-on pushed against Gideon's arse, needy and more excited than ever and Gideon nodded.

"I'm sure, if you are. I want to feel skin inside me, not latex. I want to feel Eddie." His soft words seemed to inflame Eddie and Gideon gasped as rough fingers breached him, fingers that were slick with lube, and his arse was delightfully filled. Eddie breathed heavily against the back of Gideon's neck. Gideon leaned forward and bent his knees to accommodate his shorter lover, splaying his hands against the shower wall. Eddie pushed eager fingers inside him, and Gideon rocked back in pleasure, fucking himself on them.

"Eddie, I don't need all the arse play. Just get yourself inside me. Please."

The feeling of Eddie sliding into him with his bare cock, his wet skin against his arse was like Nirvana. Gideon cried out at the sensation of hot, silky flesh impaling him as Eddie began moving with deep strokes, gripping Gideon's hips so tightly he knew he'd have bruises there. The sound of wet flesh slapping his, the intimacy of having his man deep inside him, as he grunted in pleasure and licked Gideon's skin, made Gideon's head swim as the sensations deepened. Eddie got rougher and Gideon closed his eyes and revelled in the moment. The hiss of the water, the heat of the shower steam, the groans of his lover, the sensation of being filled and wanted—it made Gideon feel like they were the only two people that mattered, that this was a moment of deep significance.

"Oh God, you feel so amazing," Eddie groaned as his cock pounded Gideon. "I know you always feel good but fuck, this is too good to bear much longer." He bit down on Gideon's shoulder and Gideon hissed with pain. "I am going to come in your arse, no barriers, that's just..." His voice tailed off as he gave a loud groan and Gideon felt the pulsing of his cock in his sensitive channel as Eddie emptied himself. The mere thought of Eddie's come inside of him made Gideon dizzy and he took one hand off the wall and fisted his cock desperately. It didn't take long and he thought he'd have come without even touching himself, the eroticism of the whole beautiful act he and Eddie were performing enough to make him orgasm. He cried out loudly as he climaxed, clenching around Eddie. His boyfriend moaned softly at the sensation of Gideon's muscles clasping his spent cock. Gideon's chest was heaving as he spurted against the shower wall and over his belly. His legs threatened to give way. The water continued to flow, showering them with warm jets, washing away the sweat and the semen from their bodies. Gideon felt a sense of loss at that. He wanted Eddie's come inside him, wanted to feel for that little bit longer Eddie's claiming of his body.

Eddie chuckled behind him as he drew out. Gideon turned to see him lean against the back shower wall, his emerald eyes with their wet, sandy lashes gazing at Gideon with a look that couldn't be mistaken. Gideon's breath stopped at that look. It was possession, lust, desire...and love.

Decision made, Gideon reached over and framed Eddie's face in his hands, leaning his forehead against his as his chest tightened at the words he was about to say.

"I love you, Eddie Tripp," he whispered. "I truly do."

Eddie's eyes widened and for a moment, Gideon had a heart-wrenching fear that he'd said the wrong thing. Then Eddie's wide mouth curved in a huge smile and his mouth found Gideon's and took possession of that too. When he finally released a gasping and breathless Gideon, his eyes were bright. They were also wet, but Gideon gave him the benefit of the doubt, pretending that it was the spray from the shower.

"I love you too," Eddie murmured. "I've never fallen so damn hard for someone in my whole life. This is it for me. *You* are it for me."

Gideon laughed in relief. "Thank God for that," he said as he reached over to turn off the water. "I thought maybe I'd moved too fast, spoiled things—"

Eddie shook his head as he drew back the screen and stepped past Gideon to get a towel. "No, that was just the perfect moment. Baring your soul after we did it bareback? I think that's a commitment to each other." He grinned as he vigorously towelled his hair dry before wrapping the towel around his waist. Gideon stepped out and did the same, marvelling at the feeling in his chest. *I just told another man I loved him. I've never said that before. It feels good. I should have done it sooner.*

"I meant it," he said quietly as he watched Eddie brush his unruly curls back. "I know it's not been long, but it just seems right, this connection you and I have. I want to see where it goes."

Eddie's face softened. "I do too. Let's just wallow in this moment before we start second guessing ourselves." His face grew mischievous. "I suggest we order something in, eat ourselves silly, then go back to bed and have more raunchy sex. How's that for a plan?"

Gideon certainly had no problem with that. "My choice of takeaway tonight," he said. "Last time you ordered that god-awful Thai stuff that looked like shit and had no redeeming qualities whatsoever. I fancy some good old-fashioned pizza. Extra olives and mushrooms. Deal?"

"Deal," Eddie agreed as he wandered out of the bathroom. Gideon watched his slim hips and pert backside disappear and grinned at himself in the mirror. This being in love thing wasn't so bad after all. For the first time in a very long time Gideon Kent was truly happy.

Chapter 16

A week later, Eddie was busy in the restaurant kitchen cleaning up. He'd volunteered to do the whole kitchen clean down himself as he was staying over again anyway and everyone else was going to some late night concert. Suddenly a pair of warm hands covered his eyes. The perfume was familiar and he grinned.

"Carmen, honey," he drawled, crumpling up the tea towel he held and throwing it in the laundry basket. "What are you still doing here so late? I thought everyone had gone home already."

The hands left his eyes and he turned around. Carmen stood there, her dark kohl-lined eyes gazing at him and the smirk on her face reminding him of a Cheshire cat.

"What? That look normally means trouble for me. What's up?"

"Oh, nothing." Carmen shook black clad shoulders. "I was just wondering how you and lover boy are doing now that you've proclaimed undying love for each other."

Eddie flushed. "Carmen," he growled. "I told you that in confidence."

Well, he'd declared it to her in a drunken, happy haze more like it, when the two of them had gone bar hopping to find the best Tequila Sunrise in London. He shuddered at the memory of going home to his own place, on one of those rare nights he did, to have a very unsympathetic Leslie put him to bed after Eddie had vomited all over his prized Christian Louboutins.

Carmen laughed, a raucous sound that sounded like a flock of cawing crows. "Honey, the staff are all clubbing together to buy you a thank-you present. We now have a boss who smiles every day, is a lot more relaxed, actually joins in at some of the socials because you're there and he's not the miserable git he used to be." She prodded Eddie's chest with a purple-tipped finger. "And that, my friend, is all *your* doing. You have been the best thing to happen to him since ever." Her tone was affectionate and there was no doubt that she meant every word she said from the look on her face.

Eddie felt warmth flush his face and a strange feeling of complete and utter satisfaction flood his body.

He nodded. "Gideon *is* a different man. He still has nightmares now but they aren't as extreme. He's still seeing his therapist, Martin, but he thinks he's doing so well, that there might only be a couple more sessions. He's sleeping better, and he hasn't had a panic attack since coming back from Norfolk." He flushed. "We're talking about moving in together but I'm not sure I'm ready for that yet."

Carmen smiled at him. "You're crazy about him, Eddie, and he you. It makes sense to stay together."

Eddie smirked "Well, you give a man hip-wrenching, mind-blowing sex and he's yours to keep forever. I know exactly how to keep my man interested."

Carmen rolled her eyes at him. "I've no doubt the two of you are heating up the sheets if that moaning the other night from his office was anything to go by. The whole damn staff knew what you two were doing."

Eddie swallowed as his face grew hotter. "We weren't doing anything," he blustered, knowing she wouldn't believe him–truth be told, neither would he. If it was the night he was thinking about, the night Gideon had taken him over his desk in a big bad boss-and-employee role play in which they'd gotten very invested. He was surprised the whole of London hadn't heard his screams of delight as Gideon 'disciplined' him. "And besides, it was after hours. No one should have been here."

No sooner were the words out than he wished he'd kept his mouth shut.

Carmen cackled again. "Busted!" she yelled, brandishing her plum-coloured fingertips at him. "It so happens me and Jerome were here, as well Andy. We'd been to the club down the road and came back to pick up Andy's train ticket home which he'd left here in his work clothes." She winked wickedly. "Jerome was tickled pink and Andy—well, he was just mortified. I had to give him a double brandy to calm his nerves." The glint in her eye belied the tall story.

Eddie scowled. "Well, they should be so lucky to have a boyfriend with a huge dick and an overwhelming desire for his young and extremely sexy boyfriend." He crossed his arms across his chest smugly as he gained momentum. "Perhaps we should be putting on a show and charging for this activity if everyone's going to start listening to us and pretending it's the latest episode of *Porn Star for Hire*."

Carmen's eyes widened in glee as she looked behind Eddie.

"Gideon's there, isn't he?" Eddie said resignedly. Carmen burst into peals of laughter as Gideon's smoky voice echoed in Eddie's ears, causing his toes to curl and his trousers to grow tight.

"Wow, Eddie, go giving away all our secrets, why don't you." Gideon's sexy drawl never failed to turn Eddie on. Gideon moved up behind his boyfriend and put his arms around his upper arms, pinning them to his side. "Maybe we should show Carmen here how we do the whole rope tying-up thing and how you beg me to bend you over and—"

Carmen let out a screech. "Oh God, someone pour bleach in my ears. That, I don't need to hear. I'm going home." She turned to Gideon. "That spreadsheet you wanted is finally finished. I had to recreate it from scratch." She flapped a hand at him. "Your new PC will be delivered in the morning, by the way. Do you think you might like to look after this one and not go all ape shit on it?"

Gideon scowled. "I suppose I might be able to do that."

Carmen sniggered. "I'll send you the bill, boss man." She grinned and reached over to give each of them a smacking kiss. "See you Thursday, boys. I have the next two days off. See you!" Carmen disappeared, leaving Eddie still captured in Gideon's arms. He didn't mind at all, he admitted to himself. There was nowhere else he'd rather be.

Gideon leaned in and nibbled his earlobe, then dragged his wet tongue down Eddie's neck. Eddie closed his eyes and shivered. Goose bumps flourished on his pale skin.

"I never get tired of doing this to you," Gideon murmured. "Making you shiver, seeing your skin all bumpy because of what I do to you. Do you have any idea what a turn-on it is to see it?"

"I can feel it," Eddie said huskily as he tilted his head to one side, giving Gideon better access to his skin. "That thing in your pants needs some TLC from the feel of it."

Gideon released him and pulled Eddie around to take his mouth in a bruising kiss that left Eddie weak kneed and wilting. He wrapped his arms around Gideon's neck as he pushed his hips against Gideon's groin. For a while there was no other sound besides lips wetly smacking together, low moans and groans and the occasional rusting of clothing as each man found his way to warm skin and leaking cocks. Hands wrapped around each other, they kissed slow and deeply and when Eddie came in Gideon's hand with a shudder and a muffled expletive, Gideon wasn't far behind. They stood, breathless and sticky and Gideon's nose wrinkled.

"Ugh. God, this room honks of us both. Sweat and jizz. Someone should bottle it."

The words didn't factor at first and then Eddie stilled, his heart literally missing a beat as he took a deep breath at the import of Gideon's words. He'd heard them but still couldn't believe it.

"What did you say?" He moved away from Gideon and tucked his limp cock back into his chef trousers. Gideon was doing the same but he looked a little confused.

"What? I said we reeked—" His voice tailed off and his eyes widened. His nostrils flared and a look of stupefaction crossed his face. Eddie couldn't stop the grin from splitting his face in half, couldn't stop his eyes stinging with sudden tears of hope and thankfulness. The same look of wonder that Eddie thought was on his face was now reflected on his lover's.

"Eddie, I can smell us." Gideon's voice was awed, whispering the words as if by doing so he hoped no one could take this incredible moment away. His eyes darkened, suspiciously wet and to Eddie, he looked…radiant. His hands were shaking as he tucked in his shirt and Eddie danced over to him in glee.

"Wow, that's awesome news. Can you still smell it? Can you smell anything else, like my aftershave or food odours?"

Gideon shook his head in a daze. "I could smell our come and your sweat—" He sniffed the air experimentally like a dog "—and I can sort of smell something spicy. It's very faint but it's there." He seemed to finally realise the breakthrough he'd just had. "Jesus, my sense of smell is coming back. Martin said it could happen, that at any time I might get it back as my brain allowed me to sense it." His face shadowed. "God, what happens if I start cooking again and can't stand the smell of meat cooking? What if I have a flashback, or a panic attack?" His voice caught and he moved towards Eddie, holding out his arms.

Eddie reached over and wrapped Gideon in his instead. "Gideon, love, stop second guessing the whole thing. It's just one milestone. Let's not get too ahead of ourselves and think of the bad stuff."

He looked around the room and felt a thrill of satisfaction when he spied a packet of chewing gum sitting on the kitchen counter top.

He opened the packet and popped a piece of gum into his mouth and started chewing.

Gideon's eyebrows waggled and he looked at Eddie with confusion. "What the hell are you doing? You don't eat gum normally."

Eddie kept chewing and motioned for Gideon to wait. Finally he finished and with a grimace, he took it out of his mouth and threw it into the nearby bin. "Ugh. I'll never understand how you can chew that muck. It's awful."

Then he bounded back to Gideon as he watched in bemusement and latched onto his mouth. "Can you taste me?" he whispered into Gideon's mouth. "Please tell me you can." His lips sought Gideon's urgently and Gideon's mouth opened as their tongues met and slicked against each other. When Eddie drew back, Gideon was looking at him with eyes that drank him in, the expression of joy and relief on his face giving Eddie his answer.

"It's faint," Gideon said breathlessly, "but I taste peppermint. I can taste you, Eddie." His voice trembled with emotion. "Jesus…" Eddie's eyes pricked with hot tears at the wonder in Gideon's tone.

"It's a start," Eddie reached up, wrapping arms around Gideon's neck and resting his forehead against Gideon's. "Let's hope it gets better. But you know what?" He kissed Gideon tenderly. "Even if this is all it is, then I'm happy for you. God, I'm happy for me. Now all that expensive aftershave I wear won't be for nothing. My man can appreciate it now."

Gideon gave a choked chuckle and bear-hugged Eddie until he thought he might pass out from lack of air. They stood together like that for a while before Gideon reluctantly pulled away and wiped his eyes with his sleeve. He tried to do it nonchalantly but Eddie knew he was having trouble suppressing tears. His tough man was just a softy deep inside.

"I guess we should finish up here, and then we're going to celebrate with a bottle of the best champagne and go to bed." Gideon's eyebrows rose suggestively. "I'd like the chance to get up close and personal with that aftershave of yours. Maybe with other things as well." He slapped Eddie's backside hard and Eddie yowled.

Gideon grinned. "Come on, gorgeous. Let's get this place spick and span and then I'll steal a bottle from the cellar. I might even let you pour it over me and lick it all off." And with that parting shot that made Eddie's cock stand up and take immediate attention, he grabbed a cloth and a bottle of spray cleaner and with a jaunty spring in his step, he disappeared over to the far counter to wipe down the counter. Eddie watched him go with a grin then picked up his own cloth.

Way to go. That man will be the death of me with his throw-away comments.

Eddie knew that Gideon's high would soon disappear as his logical mind came to terms with what had happened. Getting his sense of smell back was a huge step and Eddie hoped it would continue to get better. The fact Gideon was already worrying about his senses bringing back memories of his ordeal in the fire was troubling. Eddie hoped that it would all work out. But he knew that no matter what lay ahead for them both, he wasn't going anywhere. Gideon was stuck with him and whatever they were going through, it would be together. As he watched his boyfriend whistling as he polished and cleaned, Eddie thanked God for whatever it was had brought them both to this place.

The fact he loved the man senseless was certainly a step in the right direction. The fact he was loved back—that was a definite plus in his book.

The End

ABOUT THE AUTHOR

Susan Mac Nicol is a self-confessed bookaholic, an avid watcher of videos of sexy pole-dancing men, a self-confessed geek and nerd, and in love with her Smartphone. This little treasure is called 'the boyfriend' by her longsuffering husband, who says if it vibrated there'd be no need for him. Susan hasn't had the heart to tell him there's an app for that.

A lover of walks in the forest, theatre productions, dabbling her toes in the cold North Sea and the vibrant city of London where you can experience all four seasons in a day, she is a hater of pantomime (please don't tar and feather her), duplicitous people, bigotry and self-righteous idiots. She likes to think of herself as a 'half full' kind of gal, although sometimes that philosophy is sorely tested.

In an ideal world, Susan Mac Nicol would be Queen of England and banish all the bad people to the Never Never Lands of Wherever-Who Cares. As that's not going to happen, she contents herself with writing her HEA stories and pretending that, just for a little while, good things happen to good people.

Boroughs
Publishing Group

Did you enjoy this book? Drop us a line and say so! We love to hear from readers, and so do our authors. To connect, visit www.boroughspublishinggroup.com online, send comments directly to info@boroughspublishinggroup.com, or friend us on Facebook and Twitter. And be sure to check back regularly for contests and new releases in your favorite subgenres of romance!

Are you an aspiring writer? Check out www.boroughspublishinggroup.com/submit and see if we can help you make your dreams come true.